Return of a STREET KING

Loving My Savage 3

MEL G

SULLIVAN
PRODUCTIONS
LITERARY&FILMS

www.leosullivanpresents.com

1

JORDYN

Hearing that Ash had pulled a gun on Fatima and his own best friend, I knew for a fact that the man had gone over the deep end.

"Oh my God!" I cried, hearing glass shatter in the front room.

I began to back away from the door after hearing his angry footsteps heading in my direction.

Bam! Bam! Bam!

"Open the door, Jordyn!" he barked at me.

"Ash, please! Just leave," I begged in a shaky voice.

After a few moments of silence, I thought that he'd left or at least walked away from the door. Slowly easing out of the corner that I had tucked myself in, I cautiously neared the door to see if I could hear anything on the other side.

Boom!

A yelp escaped my mouth as the door came flying off the hinges and into the room. Ash stood glaring at me with blood-shot eyes as his chest angrily heaved up and down. My eyes zeroed in on the pistol that rested by his side. I couldn't remember the last time that I prayed as hard as I was at this very second.

"Ash, I—"

"Did you really think you would get away with doing that shit without me finding out?"

"Ash, let me—"

"Shut the fuck up! I don't want to hear shit you have to say!"

Jumping, I cowered away from him and dropped my gaze. He paced back and forth in the doorway, using his gun to scratch his temple. Neither of us said a word. Me? I was too scared to even breath the wrong way. Him? Well, I was not sure what type of twisted things were running through his head.

"What the fuck you on, Jordyn? Why did you do it? You really sat there and killed my seed, yo?" he asked. His face was hard. "My fucking seed!"

"Let me talk, Ashley!"

"Who you think you yelling at, Jordyn?" he yelled, jumping into my face. "Bitch, I'll snap your damn neck in here! I already want to put a bullet right through your trifling ass skull!"

Tears fell freely from my eyes at how harsh he was being toward me. Yeah, in the beginning he wasn't always the nicest person, but never had he been like *this*.

"Bitch? So that's where we are after all we've been through? You're disrespecting me and calling me out of my name like I mean nothing to you?"

"Yeah, that's where we are, so you can save those bullshit tears. You sat there and killed my baby, and you think I'm gon' have some sympathy for yo' ass?" He grilled me. "You sat there and lied to my face! I just want to know why you did it."

"I had to." I wept. "I didn't lie to you, Ashley. I just couldn't tell you. Do you think you would have let me go through with it if I had?"

"Hell no. I wouldn't have. What kind of sucka ass nigga you

take me for? What I look like being okay with you killing my child? *Our* child!"

"Because I didn't know if it was yours!"

It had gotten so quiet that you could hear a pin drop. I hadn't intended on just blurting that out, but I was getting tired of him yelling at me. He wouldn't even give me the opportunity to explain myself.

"Ash—"

Before my mind could register what was happening, Ash had lunged across the room at me. I didn't realize that Marcel and Fatima had both been standing right outside the door, but I was glad. Marcel managed to step in just in time and caught Ash before he could get to me.

"Move out of my way, Cello!"

"Nah, bruh! I can't let this shit go down. Let's go, Ash," Marcel said as he struggled to hold him.

"I'm not going no damn where! Move, and mind your fucking business, Marcel, before I bust a cap in yo' ass too!" Ash yelled, pushing Marcel away from him angrily.

"I'm not about to sit here and let you hurt that damn girl! You could at least hear her out, and let her explain."

"Ain't shit to explain!"

"Jordyn, get out of here, ma," Marcel told me, blocking Ash's path to me.

"She's not about to walk out of here, Marcel. The only way she's leaving is in a body bag," Ash threatened. His cold eyes stared into my soul.

"Ash, you're taking this shit too far. Calm down!" Marcel yelled and looked back over his shoulder at Faye and me. "Why the hell y'all still standing there? Leave!"

"Excuse me, but this is my house," Fatima spoke. "If anybody's leaving, it's you two."

"Now is not the time, Fatima. I don't give a damn whose

house it is!" Marcel snapped at her. "You think this man is playing about killing her? Get out!"

"Jordyn, don't walk out that door," Ash growled at me. "Cello, I love you, bruh, but I'll beat yo' ass if you don't back up off me."

"It is what it is then, bro," Marcel told him, not backing down.

I might not have had the chance to witness Marcel in action, but I had seen Ash, and I would have been out of my mind to ever bet against him. Fatima could argue back and forth with Marcel if she wanted to, but I was taking this opportunity to get the hell away from here. I bolted from the room without another thought. Ash and Marcel could be heard tussling behind me, and I was sure that I was going to have to pay Fatima for the damage they were doing to her place.

"Jordyn!" Fatima called, running right behind me. "Wait!"

"For what? You heard Cello. That man is going to kill me," I said, looking around nervously for the first set of keys I could find. "I'm not about to sit around and wait for it to happen."

"Well, I'm going with you. You're not leaving me here alone with them," she said, grabbing her phone and keys and rushing out the door behind me. "Where are we even going? I left my purse and everything else inside."

I realized I had done the same thing. "I don't know, Faye, and I really don't care. I just need to get away from here."

Fatima's phone sounded off throughout the car, and she held it up to show me the caller ID.

"What, Marcel?"

"Where are y'all?" he asked.

"Why? I'm not about to tell you, especially not with that lunatic around you," Fatima told him.

"For your information, he left out right after y'all did,"

Marcel stated matter of factly. "How long do you think it's going to take for him to catch up with her?"

"Can't you talk to him and tell him what's going on? This is all your fault in the first place. Had you not opened your big mouth before you knew what was going on, this wouldn't be happening."

"Girl, you better gon' somewhere with that. Had your girl been straight up from the jump, all this bullshit could have been avoided. Now, where are y'all?"

"I don't know." She sighed a breath of frustration before looking around. "We're on Third, heading toward University."

"Look, tell Jo to go to my spot. I'm on my way there now."

"Your spot? Nah, we're good."

"I'm not asking you, Fatima. Get there now unless you want your niece's blood on your hands." His voice boomed through the speaker before he disconnected the call.

LYING ON MY BACK AND STARING UP AT THE CEILING, I WAS tired of hiding out at Marcel's house. I had been here for the past three days, and Marcel was adamant about not letting me leave until this blew over, and Ash calmed down. How long did it take for somebody to calm down? I knew Ash knew what happened because Marcel told me that he had finally managed to get him to sit still long enough to listen.

According to Marcel, after finding out what happened, that only made the situation worse. Ash was going crazy and was killing almost everything in his path. He already had a lot of pressure on him, and my situation didn't help not one bit.

Andre's mom had even called me. She was scared out of her mind because she figured I had something to do with the "strange men" that had been looking for her punk ass son and staking out her house.

My head snapped toward the bedroom door after hearing it open, and my breath caught in my throat at the sight of Ash standing there. His eyes were bloodshot red, and the pungent smell of weed greeted me before he did.

Slowly pulling myself to a seated position, I cautiously moved to the opposite side of the bed as he came and sat at the foot. The last time I saw him, he was trying to kill me, so I wasn't sure what to expect from the sudden visit.

After about a good twenty minutes of silence, I realized that he didn't plan on saying anything, and I decided that I would speak first.

"Are you just going to sit there?"

He glanced over his shoulder at me briefly before turning back around and choosing not to answer my question. What was the point of him coming if he was only going to ignore me?

"So you're not going to say anything? It's been almost a week, Ash. Where have you been?" I questioned. "I know you talked to Cello already."

Marcel said that it was best if I gave Ash some time to digest the news of what happened with Andre, but those days felt like years. Since the beginning of our relationship, Ash and I had damn near been glued at the hip. It took me by surprise at how attached we were to each other. I wasn't feeling his little disappearing act.

"I needed to think," he finally said, sighing as he rubbed his hands down his face.

"And you had to go ghost on me to do that? You could have at least called, Ashley," I nagged. "I was driving myself crazy worrying about you. You already know how much shit is going on."

"Exactly. Which is why I don't need the added bullshit from you," he barked.

My eyes bucked at his harsh words. I knew he was upset about me not telling him about what Dre had done or the abortion. What else was I supposed to do, though? My first thought *had* been to go straight to Ash, but the more I thought about it, the more I realized how much of a potential disaster that could turn out to be. Ash had already been out here running loose like a madman, and there was no telling what that news would have made him do.

After much prayer and battling with myself, I decided that I was going to just let karma take care of Andre and tried my best to put that night and those memories to the back of my head. I had no clue that everything was going to come crashing down on me like it had.

"So I'm bullshit to you now?"

"Man, don't be putting words in my mouth," he said, frowning. "Everything that's going on is bullshit. What yo' ass did was bullshit. You kept this shit from me, Jordyn. All you had to do was open your damn mouth and tell me! What was so damn hard about that?"

"I couldn't!" I cried out, frantically shaking my head.

"What the hell do you mean you couldn't? I don't want to hear that! What? You trying to protect that motherfucker or something?"

My face instantly displayed a look of disgust at his question. "Why the hell would I want to protect him? I hate him!"

"Then what the hell, Jordyn?" he asked, not understanding my reasoning.

My head dropped as tears continued to fall freely from my eyes. "I knew you would look at me differently if you found out. Ash, I know you don't understand, and what I did was probably wrong in your eyes, but it's not like I asked for any of this. I couldn't keep that baby," I told him. "If it had been his, I—"

"But what if it was mine?" he yelled, shooting to his feet and starting to pace in front of me. "Every time I think about it, I want to wring your damn neck. I mean that shit too. I want to literally put hands on you, and that's not something I want to do because I love yo' ass. This is too much right now. I have enough fucked up shit being thrown at me. I can't do this. Maybe we need to chill before this gets out of hand."

My face frowned up as my head cocked to the side. I must not have been hearing him correctly. For a minute, I forgot all about being sad and that damn crying because it sounded to me like he was trying to break up with me or something.

"Come again? Chill? I'm sorry, but I don't know what the hell *chill* means. I get that you're mad, and you have every right to be, but don't try to shut me out. I can't take back what I did, and even if I could, I wouldn't. As far as that *chilling* bullshit you talking, ain't no chilling. We're together. Just like you tell me. You don't have a choice in the matter."

"Don't do this, ma. Let's not make this shit harder than what it needs to be. We tried, baby girl, but this ain't working for me. Maybe I should have been cut things off. I can't focus on shit out in the streets and yo' ass at the same time. This is better for both of us. It's already obvious that you evidently can't even trust me to be your man and be there for you, so what's the point of us even doing this? You can go back to living your life and doing you, and I'll do the same."

"Okay. See, I feel like you playing with me right now. You really have me fucked up, so let me break it down for you on how this shit is about to go. I'm going to give you a couple more days to get your mind right. Then we're going to get this shit together. I need you just as much as you need me. I know like hell you didn't think you could *force* me into a relationship, make me fall for you, and then just say 'fuck it.' You ready to call it quits? Nah, shit don't work like that. *I* don't work like that. What you're going to do is get the hell out, and take your behind home."

"Look—"

"Ain't no 'look.' Like I said, we're not over. I'll let you have your little *moment* to handle your business and get your mind right, but that's it. There's no such thing as over as far as I'm concerned. While you're taking this time of reflection, don't get out there being stupid and thinking it's okay to entertain these bitches."

"Yo, what the fuck? I'm breaking up with you, man. This shit dead."

"Nah, the only thing dead is you if you think I'm playing with you. I tried being patient and letting you digest all this, because I know it's not easy, but you're trippin'. Now, once again, get out. I'll see you later," I said, opening the door and waiting for him to make his exit.

"Man, whatever. I'm not about to go back and forth with you," he said, shaking his head and heading to the door.

"Neither am I with you. I said what I said. You can take me for a joke if you want to," I asserted right before he walked out of the room.

Honestly, I felt like he was only looking for an out, and this gave him one, but Ash could try me if he wanted to. He was going to witness a completely different side of Jordyn.

MARCEL

"Hey, daddy's baby." I smiled, staring down at my phone as I watched Heaven on the screen, cheesing into the camera and babbling incoherently. "What you talking about, mama? You miss me?"

"Da Da Da Da," she excitedly sang, clapping her chubby hands together.

"Daddy will see you in a minute, Stank." My mom's face came back into view of the camera. "I won't be too late today, Ma. I just have one more appointment, and then I'm wrapping things up."

"She's fine, Marcel. We ain't stuntin' you. Us girls are enjoying ourselves. Just come in the morning," my mom told me.

"Ma, why you be trying to hog my baby?" I jokingly questioned. "You be trying to hold her hostage like you don't be wanting her to come home."

"Because you be trying to cut into our fun time." She pouted. "It's Friday. Aren't you supposed to be going out with

Ash or something. Better yet, go fix yourself up, and take my daughter-in-law out somewhere nice."

"Ma," I groaned, rolling my eyes. "What I told you?"

"A bunch of bullshit," she answered, cocking her head to the side. "Stop dwelling on stuff, and move on. You love her, and she loves you, so what's the problem?"

"Man, it's not that easy."

"That's because you're making it harder than what it has to be. You better hurry up before someone else comes along and snatches her up," she urged.

The idea of Fatima being with someone else wasn't an image I wanted in my head. My jaw tightened just at the thought. I'd kill any nigga who tried to step to her. That probably was extreme, but I didn't care.

"I hear you, Ma, but I gotta dip. My next client here," I said to her after hearing a light knock at my door, ending our call. "Aye, come in!"

"Hey, baby."

My head snapped up, and I instantly frowned. "Mariah, what the hell are you doing here?" I asked, grilling her.

That chick had lost her damn mind by coming down to my place of business. I already had to block her after she kept blowing up my phone. She was straight bugging. I hadn't been fooling with her since the day I cut things off between us and left her crib.

The woman wasn't taking no for an answer and couldn't seem to get it through her head that there was nothing between us.

"Mariah, answer my damn question? Why would you bring your behind down to my shop?"

"Because you haven't been answering my calls, and I wanted to see you. We need to talk," she said, approaching me and reaching out to touch my chest.

Reflexively, I knocked her hands away from me and took a step back. "Aye, you need to bounce, ma. I got shit to do, and I'm expecting a client."

"Here I am," she announced, posing.

"Yo, what type of fucking games are you trying to play? I don't have time for this shit," I fussed.

"I'm not trying to play any games, Marcel. Baby, I just—"

"Stop calling me your damn baby." I snapped. "You need to go."

"But what about my tattoo?"

"Forget that damn tattoo. Leave, Mariah, and don't bring your ass back down here," I told her, escorting her to the door of my studio.

As soon as I opened it, Jordyn was standing there with her fist up, preparing to knock. Dropping her hand back down to her side, she looked back and forth between Mariah and I with a raised brow. I already knew what she was thinking, and I was praying her crazy behind didn't say or do anything.

"Bye, Mariah," I told her, trying to hurry and push her past Jordyn.

"I'll see you later," she said, leaving my studio reluctantly.

"No, you won't, and don't come back down here. I'm serious."

"Well, damn." Jordyn snickered.

Mariah turned her sights on Jordyn and looked her up and down. "And who the hell are you?"

"A problem you don't want, sweetie." Jordyn laughed. "Keep it moving."

If Mariah knew like I did, she would take heed to that warning, and go on about her business. Jordyn was spazzing out on everybody lately since she and Ash had been beefing. Mariah was liable to get killed in here. I was glad when Mariah finally decided to take the hint and stormed away.

"What was that about?" Jordyn asked me.

"Nothing, ma. What's up?"

She followed behind me back into my studio and leaned against my workstation.

"I see your boy hasn't been taking any clients this week. Have you talked to him?" she questioned.

"Yeah, I talked to him," I answered, keeping it short.

"What's he been doing? He's still not answering any of my calls, and he changed the code to the gate."

"I mean, I don't know, Jordyn. I guess he's been handling business."

"You guess? Okay, and?" she probed.

"And nothing, Jordyn. I'm done getting in the middle of y'all's mess. That's what almost got me shot the last time. I think I've learned my lesson," I told her, shaking my head.

"But—"

"Nope. I'm minding my business. You need anything else?" I asked, packing up my belongings.

"Ugh!" She huffed, stomping her midget ass away.

Jordyn could be mad at me all she wanted to. She would get over it. Jo was my girl, but we weren't *that* cool for me to be getting shot or beat up over. Didn't nobody have time to be fighting Ash's big, trigger-happy ass. They could have that.

After leaving the shop, I shot by Ma Dukes' spot to check on baby girl, and then I was headed to the crib to get ready for tonight. Ash had hit me up because he wanted to step out, and I was down. It had been a minute since the two of us were really able to chill out and relax, and we had the perfect relaxation spot.

CHILLING IN OUR PRIVATE SECTION, I VIBED TO THE MUSIC AS

strippers flooded our area, breaking their necks at the opportunity to get at Ash. That smooth ass nigga was eating all the attention up too. Bruh was definitely on one tonight. Usually, he was the one sitting back and observing the crowd while I was busy wilding out. Not at the moment. He was straight cutting up.

I shook my head as I watched him fire up what had to be about his fifth blunt. I had long ago tapped out on him and was content with sipping from my cup of Hennessy. If his goal was to get fucked up, he was well on his way.

"Aye, man. You might want to slow down before your ass be passed out somewhere," I expressed.

"That's the plan," he said, exhaling a cloud of smoke into the air.

"This not even like you. What's up with you, bruh?"

"What? Nothing's up with me. Man, I'm chilling, trying to enjoy all these bad ass females," he said, smacking the ass of the closest stripper to him and pulling her down onto his lap, causing her to giggle.

"Come on, Ash. I know when something's fucking with you," I called him out.

"The only thing fucking with me is you sitting here trying to have a heart to heart in the middle of the club, messing up my high and shit."

"I'm just trying to check on your ass, hoe."

"Well, don't. I'm good. Fuck Jordyn."

I sat back and side-eyed him, laughing. "Who said anything about Jordyn?"

Just like he knew me, I knew Ash like the back of my hand, so I already knew that baby girl was on his mind heavy. He could front all he wanted to, but he was missing her. His stubborn behind was just too bull-headed to admit it. Even though I told Jordyn that I was staying out of it, I had attempted to talk some sense into Ash on multiple occasions. I understood his reasons for cutting things off with her, but it was also bogus as hell if you asked me.

"You don't seem to be enjoying yourself, baby," one of the strippers said to me, running her hands all over my chest.

"I'm just chilling, ma," I told her, turning my cup up to my lips.

"Nuh uh. Come here, Cinnamon," she said, calling one of her girls over. "We need to cheer his fine ass up."

I leaned back in my seat and allowed them to do their thing. I was not going to lie. I was enjoying the visual of them both seductively touching and grinding all over each other. I took my eyes off them long enough to see old girl who was sitting on Ash's lap being yanked back by her hair and slung to the ground.

"Jordyn? Aye, chill!" I yelled, pushing the chicks away from me and rushing over to them.

Jordyn had come out of nowhere and caught us all off guard. She was going to town on the stripper that had started to get a little too touchy-feely with Ash, while Fatima stood close by, daring anyone to try to jump in.

"Jo! Let that girl go, man!" I yelled as I tried to pull them apart.

"Let me go, Cello! Fuck her! This hoe sitting on my man's lap like she belongs there. Bitch, I'll show you what happens when you touch what's mine!" Jordyn bellowed, refusing to loosen her grip on the girl's hair.

"Somebody, get this bitch off me!"

"Man, what the hell you doing, Jordyn? Why you even here?" Ash yelled once he finally snapped out of it and realized what was going on.

"Why am I here? That's all you have to say to me after ignoring me for two whole weeks? Then you have the audacity to be up here feeling all over some bitch!" she yelled, standing over where he was still sitting with an unamused expression resting on his face.

"Ma, I can do that. I'm single as fuck, or did you forget?" he asked, turning his cup up to his lips and downing the dark liquor.

Jordyn laughed to herself as she stared off into space for a minute before turning back to him. "Nah, did *you* forget me telling you that I'd dead your ass if you even *thought* you were," she replied, slapping the cup from his hand and mushing him in the center of his forehead.

He slapped her hand away from him and jumped to his feet, towering over her. "Don't put your fucking hands on me, girl," he growled at her.

Wham!

The loud slap sounded off throughout the section and caused everyone to go silent as we watched Ash's eyes grow dark. I just knew it was about to be a murder in there. I watched his fists clench at his side as he struggled to contain the beast inside him. By then, security had already made their way over to our section.

"Go home, Jordyn," Ash coldly ordered before resuming his seat and pulling a new chick down onto his lap.

The girl hesitantly looked from Ash to Jordyn. She was obviously not sure if that was the right move. After watching Jordyn put the paws on her friend, I was sure she wasn't trying to be next.

"Jordyn, come on," Fatima begged after Jordyn struggled against the security and was ready to turn up on them too. "He's not worth it, Jo. Let's just leave."

"Oh, I'm gon' leave alright. I can see myself out," she said, snatching away from the bouncer. "He wants to play with me, but he must not know I'm the queen of games. We can play all day. Oooh, Ash. I swear to God you about to regret this shit."

Her eyes were on Ash the entire time she made her way from our section until she was out of sight. I wasn't going to lie. Jordyn had me a little shook. That look in her eyes was one that I'd witnessed plenty of times before, except it was usually on Ash.

Shaking my head at him, I got up to go make sure that the ladies were good. I knew Ash wasn't in his right mind because there was no way he would have handled Jordyn like that had he been sober.

"Oh shit!" I cringed.

I walked out just in time to see Jordyn throwing the steel bat she held in her hands to the ground and walking over to Fatima's car to pull something else from the trunk. Cringing at the sight in front of me, I knew it was about to be some shit. I was shocked at the damage she had done to Ash's truck. I was frozen in place for a minute. That truck was his damn baby, and she had busted his shit up.

"Jordyn, let's go! Somebody's already called the police," Fatima said to her.

"I don't care. They can call 'em. This man got me fucked up!"

It wasn't until I noticed the can of gasoline in her hands that I finally snapped out of it. I rushed over to her and snatched the canister from her hand just as she began dumping its contents through the broken window and onto the front seat of the truck.

"Girl, are you crazy!" I barked at her. "What the hell you doing?"

"What does it look like?"

Jordyn's ass was Houdini out this bitch or something, because before I knew what was happening, a lighter appeared out of nowhere, and she flicked it through the window. It didn't take long for the flames to start, and I could hear sirens in the distance.

"What the fuck!" I heard Ash's voice.

Ash pushed his way through the crowd, making a beeline straight in Jordyn's direction. She stared him down the entire time and was unfazed by his anger. She was ready for war. Before he could make it to her, two officers approached with their Tasers already drawn and aimed at her.

"Hands behind your back, ma'am," one of them yelled.

"Yo, look at my car!" Ash yelled, examining the damage. "Have you lost your damn mind?"

"I sure the fuck have!" she screamed back. "And what?"

They both weren't paying either of the officers any damn attention. I was just praying that they both didn't get arrested out here.

"Ma'am," an officer barked with more authority in his tone. "Hands behind your back! You are under arrest."

Another slowly approached her with cuffs already in his hands. I was surprised she didn't resist when he slapped them on her wrists.

"Aye, bruh. Get your hands off her," Ash vented, moving toward them, causing them to immediately raise their guns in his direction.

"Sir, we're going to need for you to stand back."

"Fuck that! What y'all arresting her for?" he barked.

They looked past him toward the burning car. They were probably wondering if that fool was blind or something. Why did he think they were arresting her?

"Sir, she's being arrested for assault, disturbing the peace, destruction of property, and arson," the officer advised him, running down the long laundry list of offenses.

Ash mugged Jordyn as they hauled her off to one of the

police cruisers with Fatima frantically running to her car to follow behind them. What a night this turned out to be.

❦

THE SECOND JORDYN STEPPED FOOT OUT OF THE JAIL, SHE tried to turn and go right back inside, but I stopped her before she could.

"Nope. Bring your lil' ass on," I advised her, grabbing her arm and turning in the direction of where my car was waiting.

"Why are you here, Marcel?"

"A 'thank you' would be nice."

"Too bad you're not getting one."

"Ma, I don't know what you got an attitude with me for," I said to her, opening the door for her to get inside.

Fatima was in the car waiting for us and threw her arms around her the second she was inside. They were acting like she had been gone for years instead of just a couple days.

"Where are we going?" Fatima asked after noticing that I was heading in the opposite direction of her apartment.

Jordyn's eyes cut over at me, and she already knew what was up. "Look, if you bonded me out just so that nigga can kill me, y'all can go ahead and get it over with. I'm not trying to be tied up like his other bitch," she smartly expressed, rolling her eyes.

"Ain't nobody about to kill you," I assured her.

"We both know that's a lie."

I didn't think that Ash planned on killing her, but there was no telling where his head was. "I mean, he's pissed, but what do you expect? Jo-Jo, your lil' ass is too pretty to be *this* damn crazy," I said, shaking my head. "Did you have to set the man's car on fire?"

"Yep, and I'd do it again," she declared, turning to look out the window.

When we finally pulled up at Ash's house, I cut the engine and got out. Neither of them made a move to follow me.

"Jordyn."

"I'm not going in there, Marcel."

"Jo—"

Before I could get my sentence out, the passenger door was being snatched open, and Jordyn was yanked from the car. I quickly looked over the roof of my car in time to see Ash toss Jordyn over his shoulder and stalk back toward his front door.

"Ahh! Put me down!" she yelled, beating her fists against his back, but her blows didn't seem to faze him.

"Ash, please put her down," Fatima begged.

"Ash—"

The door slammed in our faces, and I could hear the locks click into place. Fatima and I exchanged looks, and I saw the fear in her eyes. Hell, she had a right to be scared. It wasn't looking too good for Jordyn.

ASH

I struggled to keep Jordyn in my arms as she fought against me. I thought that the couple of days I let her ass sit in that jail would give me some time to cool off, but I was wrong. I was still just as pissed as I was the night that all that shit went down. I couldn't believe Jordyn.

It was no secret that baby girl wasn't wrapped too tight, but I had underestimated just how off in the head she really was. Her popping up on us at the club and fighting the stripper was one thing, but to fuck my truck up *and* set that bitch on fire was taking it too far. The fact that her eyes held absolutely zero fear as she did all this let me know that I for sure had found my match.

"Bitch, let me go!" Jordyn yelled as she hit me in the back of the head.

Making my way over to the couch, I roughly tossed her from my shoulder and body slammed her onto the couch. She popped back up and started wildly swinging at me, but I blocked her blows.

"What the hell you wildin' for? You better keep your hands to yourself! I'm the one that should be pissed," I barked. "You set my truck on fire!"

"Fuck you and that truck!" she screamed. "I'm feeling real Left Eye-*ish* today, and I'm tempted to set this bitch on fire too!"

"And I'll body yo' ass," I replied. "Keep playing with me, and I'm gon' send you to meet her."

"Do it then," she demanded, trying to connect her fists wherever she could.

Placing one of my large hands around her neck, I roughly pushed her back down onto the couch and held her there.

"Get off me!" she screamed, clawing at my arms with her nails.

"Calm your ass down, and maybe I will!" I yelled.

"Let me go! I fucking hate you!" She cried hysterically.

"Shut up! I better not ever hear you say that shit again," I growled through gritted teeth, tightening my grip.

"You're hurting me." She barely managed to get her words out with my massive hands cutting off her oxygen.

Releasing her throat, I gripped her wrists in my hands and slammed them against the couch above her head. "I'm not playing with you, Jordyn. Don't ever say no shit like that to me!"

"Why not? It's the truth! I hate you, Ashley!"

"Jordyn," I called out in a warning tone.

"You turned your back on me and walked away. I needed you, Ash, and you weren't there!" she screamed in my face with tears pouring from her eyes.

"How could I be there for you if you wouldn't let me?" I raised my voice. "You want to be mad and keep crying about me not being there, but *you're* the one who stopped that!"

"And I've apologized for not coming to you. I wish I would have handled that the right way, but I can't go back and change it. That still doesn't change the fact that even after you *knew* what happened, you did exactly what I knew you would and still left me, Ashley. Do you know how that made me feel? You sat there and made me feel like all of this was my fault. You think I asked for any of this to happen?"

I felt like shit as I listened to her and watched her cry. She was right. After I had calmed down enough and let Marcel explain everything that she told him and Fatima, I should have gone straight to her. Instead, I turned my back on Jordyn all because my pride wouldn't allow me to be there for her.

It wasn't sitting well with me that it was the second time that someone had caused harm to her, and I wasn't there to do anything about it. As her man, it was my job to protect her, and I had dropped the ball.

"You think I blame you? Really, Jordyn?"

"Why else would you be treating me like this, Ashley? You acted as if I was nothing to you! You humiliated me in front of everyone in that damn club like I was some random bitch off the streets," she cried out. "It's cool, though. I'm done begging you. If you don't want to be with me because of this, fine. You can go on about your bullshit life without me in it. I won't ever bother you again. Believe that."

"Ma, I'm sorry," I groaned, releasing her and sitting up.

She took that as the opportunity to get away from me and stood to her feet. "That's one thing you're right about. I'm done with this and your *sorry* ass. Like you said, we just need to end this shit because one of us is bound to end up dead or in jail."

"Jordyn, don't—"

Wham!

She tried to rush away after striking me across the face, but I caught her and roughly pushed her into the wall.

"I'm not going to tell you again about putting your damn

hands on me," I growled close to her face, grabbing her cheeks roughly in my hand and kissing her lips hard.

"Move, Ash," she croaked, fighting against me. "I don't want to be here! I hate you."

"What did I just tell you about that?" I asked, staring into her eyes. "You don't hate me, Jordyn. You love me just as much as I love you."

"No, I don't," she defiantly responded through tears. "Not anymore."

"Yes, you do," I confidently stated, biting down on her lip. "You could never hate me, Jo."

"Ash, let me go." She weakly attempted to free herself.

Gazing into her eyes, I slowly let go of her arms, but stayed on alert just in case she decided to swing on my ass again. She stood staring back at me with her chest heaving up and down. I knew Jordyn, and she didn't really want to leave.

Even though I was the one that made the choice to stay away, I had been missing my woman. It wasn't easy keeping my distance. I constantly battled with whether I should go to her or not, but my stubborn ways always stopped me.

"I don't want you to go, Jo," I told her, blocking her body between myself and the wall. "I want you here with me. I *need* you here with me."

"Why? You're single, remember?"

"Baby girl, you know I didn't mean that shit," I admitted, moving my lips to her neck and grazing her skin.

"I don't know anything other than what you said."

"Well, what did I *just* say?" I asked, caressing between her legs.

"Stop, Ash. Do you think sex is going to fix this?" She fussed as I unbuttoned her pants and worked them down her legs.

"No. I know for a fact it's not, but I missed you and I need you," I said, lifting her into my arms.

That hard act that she was still holding on to was just a front. The pool of moisture between her legs was telling me that she wanted me just as much. She wrapped her legs tightly around my waist as I freed my man from my sweats and rammed my dick inside of her.

It had been too long since I'd felt her inner sanctum, and my knees buckled at the feeling of her gushy walls pulling me in deeper. I could spend the rest of my life inside of her and be just fine. Between her legs was home. Jordyn was home.

Frames from the wall fell to the floor as I roughly fucked her, giving her all of me, and she was taking it like a champ. Her mouth dropped open as she struggled to catch her breath and held onto my shoulders for dear life.

"Fuck! I missed you so much," I moaned into her neck, cradling her close to me.

"Oh, God! I missed you too," she cried out, digging her nails into my shoulders.

"You still hate me?" I grunted, gripping her hips tighter in my hands and beginning to grind deep inside her nice and slow.

"No! God no, Ashley! Shit! I love you so much, baby! Please don't stop," she begged. "Fuck!"

Boom. Boom. Boom.

The constant beating at the door didn't break my rhythm. We were both in a zone. Jordyn began bouncing wildly on my dick, and I knew she was close to the edge, and so was I. Grabbing the back of her neck, I brought her lips to mine and forced my tongue in her mouth, nastily kissing her as I felt her juices begin to drench me. I was right behind her, releasing what felt like buckets of cum inside her.

She collapsed into my chest, trying to catch her breath as I walked us back over to the couch and took a seat with her still on my lap.

"You know I'm still fucking you up about my truck, right?"

✺

INHALING THE STRONG KUSH INTO MY LUNGS, I ALLOWED the gas to invade my system as I passed the blunt next to me to Marcel. We both sat without speaking a word, letting the silence settle around us. I knew he had a million questions to ask me, but he kept them to himself for the time being.

"Ain't that your boy right there?" Marcel asked, pointing across the street.

Taking another look at the picture in my hand, a sneaky smile crept across my face. After sitting outside in this car for the past three hours or so, I was glad that he decided to finally bring his punk ass home.

"Yep. Let's roll," I said, pulling on my handle and hopping out the car.

The slamming of my door grabbed his attention and caused him to glance over his shoulder in our direction. Even with the distance between us, I could see his ass shaking like a stripper as he watched us approach.

"Mr. Andre, you're just the person I need to see." I smirked.

My eyes zoomed in on his hand as I caught him about to reach under his shirt. It was too bad he wasn't quick enough. Crashing the butt of my pistol against his temple, I sent him falling into the door and watched as blood trickled down his forehead.

"Ahh shit!" he yelled out like a little bitch.

"Shut up. That wasn't shit," Marcel mocked, snatching Dre's piece from his waistband and examining the gun. "What the hell you expected to do with this lil' shit?"

"Man, look. I don't have nothing but a few dollars in my pocket," he admitted.

I slapped him with my gun again before yanking him up by the front of his shirt. "Don't insult me. You know exactly why we're here, and it damn sure ain't to rob your broke ass," I growled. "You like taking shit that don't belong to you, right?"

"I don't know—"

His head snapped back as I stuck him again. "Bitch, didn't I just say don't insult me? Keep playing dumb if you want to. Unlock the fucking door," I ordered, pushing him toward it.

He nervously fumbled with the keys in his hands, trying to find the right one. I was growing impatient and felt like he was only trying to buy himself some time. Pressing my gun against his temple, I eyed him without saying a word. That cold steel sure helped him locate the right key with a quickness, and we were inside in no time.

Marcel took a quick look around outside to be sure that no one saw anything and closed the door behind us. Pushing Dre toward the couch, I motioned for him to take a seat and stood in front of him.

"Where's your girl?" I questioned, glancing around the living room.

"She's not here, man," he cried out. "She and my daughter at her mama house."

"Lucky for them." I shrugged and took a seat on the coffee table.

"I'm about to go see what they got in this bitch to eat," Marcel said, heading to the kitchen.

"Fool, really?"

"Yes, really. It ain't like you offered to feed my ass," he commented. "We been sitting out there forever, and I'm hungry as hell."

"Hurry up," I barked. "And don't be in there touching all on shit."

"I know that. Just handle that, so we can bounce," he said before disappearing.

I shook my head, trying to figure out why I brought

Marcel's behind with me in the first place. I had intended on riding out solo, but he insisted on coming. Had I known he was going to be working my nerves, I would have left him where he was.

My eyes focused back on Andre as he cowered in front of me. I stared at him as I tried to figure out what the hell Jordyn ever saw in that clown. Knowing Jordyn, I couldn't even picture her being with someone like him. Her little feisty behind was too damn strong for a bitch like this. I could spot a fuckboy from a mile away, and he was definitely certified.

"You know," I stated, sitting my gun down beside me and clasping my hands together in front of me. "I've been playing this moment out in my head for a good lil' minute, trying to decide how I wanted to handle your bitch ass. At first, I figured I'd just hit you with one up top and keep it moving, but I figured that would be too easy. Then I thought about chaining you to the back of my bike and hitting a hundred down the highway until your blood painted the streets. I mean, I'm still considering that since I've righteously been wanting to try that shit."

His eyes watered as he sat listening to me go into detail about how I planned on ending his pathetic life.

"Man, I'm sorry," he cried out, dropping his head.

"Sorry for what? What could you possibly have to be sorry for?" I inquired. "Is it because you completely ignored my warning about staying the fuck away from my woman? Or maybe it's the fact that you not only disregarded that warning, but you committed the ultimate no-no. Bitch, you could lose your life for less fucking with me, but that shit you pulled? Yeah, I plan on hand delivering you to the devil myself."

"Listen, I didn't—"

"Aye, forget all that." I waved him off. "Ain't shit you really need to be saying to me. Stand yo' ass up."

"Huh?"

"Did I stutter?" I asked, snatching him up and sending my fist crashing into his nose. "I want you to take this ass whooping like a man."

I didn't allow him time to think before I started raining blows on him. At first, he tried to at least put up some type of fight, but the powerful blows I was hitting him with stopped him from doing much of anything. Every punch was landing with so much force that I could feel his bones breaking under my fists.

At that point, all he could really do was guard his face as best as he could, and even that wasn't helping. Blood was leaking all over the place, and that only pushed me to go harder.

He opened his mouth in an attempt to speak, but I punched him dead in it, knocking a few of his teeth out in the process. I had completely zoned out and was still going to work on him when I felt someone touch my arm. I turned around ready to fuck somebody else up but chilled once I realized that it was only Marcel.

"Damn." He whistled, looking down at Andre's beaten frame as he groaned in pain. "You sure the man ain't already dead? I doubt if you gon' need old dude and nem."

"His bitch ass still breathing," I said, kicking Andre in the side, flipping him over onto his back. "Send them on in."

"Man, just kill me. Please," he begged before coughing up blood onto the beige carpet.

"Hold down, my boy. We gon' get to all that. Why you so impatient?" I asked right as Marcel came back in with three big, burly ass dudes in tow. "First, I got a few of my boys that I want you to meet. Dre, meet Tyrone, Dee, and Dino. Fellas, meet your new bitch."

Dino rubbed his hands together as he stared down at Dre.

Andre's head snapped in my direction as his eyes widened in horror. He knew what time it was.

"Y'all boys don't have too much fun." I smiled wickedly before turning to the three. "Make sure you don't kill his bitch ass. Leave that to me."

"You got it, boss. We gon' take *real* good care of him."

4

JORDYN

"Oh my God, Jordyn!" Fatima sucked her teeth at me. "Can you please answer that dang phone, or put it on silent. It's about to work my nerves."

Muting the ringer, I placed it face down back on the counter. "It's nobody but Dre's worrisome ass mammy. She's been blowing me up all morning."

"What the hell does she want?" Fatima turned her lip up, frowning.

"Hell if I know. I didn't bother to answer. I don't have anything to say to her or anyone else associated with that piece of shit," I replied.

"Well, block her then."

"Girl, I did. She keeps calling me from different numbers. I'm thinking about just changing my number altogether," I told her, turning my attention back to the TV. "Turn that up, Faye."

I listened as the news reporter struggled through the breaking news report.

"Twenty-four-year-old Andre Johnson has been identified as the victim of a gruesome murder that took place some time on Sunday

evening. Johnson's dismembered remains were discovered by his girl-friend at her home on the 1800 block of Ensley. Authorities are not disclosing the girlfriend's identity. At this time, there are no suspects in custody. The police are asking that if you have any information that may be vital to this investigation, please contact the Birmingham Police Department."

Fatima and I both sat with our mouths hanging wide open in utter disbelief and shock of what we were hearing. We locked eyes, and I knew that we were both thinking the same thing. I knew exactly who the damn culprit behind it was. Snatching my phone from the table, I hurried to dial Ash and waited as he took forever to answer.

"Talk to me, baby." His deep voice flowed through the line.

"Did you do it?" I asked, skipping the pleasantries.

"How you just gon' call throwing out questions like I know what you're talking about. I do a lot of shit, baby. What are you speaking of?"

"Don't be smart. *Andre*, Ashley. Did you do it?"

He chuckled. "You're funny, shorty," he said, ignoring my question. "I'll see you later. I'll be home a little late tonight."

Just like that, he ended our call and left me sitting here looking stupid. I wasn't crazy. I didn't need to hear it come out of his mouth to know that he was responsible. Thinking back to the details, I cringed at the visual that it had put in my head. If Ash was capable of what they were saying was done to Dre, he was a lot more twisted in the head than I thought.

"What did he say?" Fatima questioned.

"Not a damn thing. All he said was that he'd see me later, and it was going to be late."

Shaking her head, she chuckled to herself. "Jordyn, if I haven't already said it before, I'm going to say it again. Ash's ass is bat-shit crazy. You better be careful messing with that man.

Andre deserved what he got, but that was still some sick shit. I bet that's why his mama been blowing you up."

"Oh damn," I said, completely forgetting about Dre's mom. "You right, but why the hell would she be calling me. I don't have anything to do with any of that."

"I don't know, but you might want to answer the next time she calls just to see what she says," she suggested. "She probably just trying to see if you heard the news already."

"I don't know what makes her think I care about anything dealing with his ass," I said, frowning up my face.

"So you don't feel anything about hearing what happened to Dre?" Fatima asked, curiously.

"Nope," I answered without a second thought. "That bastard got what he deserved. I just wish Ash would have let me in on it."

"Well, damn, bitch. Ash done turned your little ass out. You just a regular old gangsta now, huh?" Fatima laughed.

⚜

BALANCING MY PHONE ON MY SHOULDER, I SIFTED THROUGH my keys, trying to find the key to Grams' house.

"You should have waited on me. I was coming by this morning anyway," Fatima told me.

Finally getting the door unlocked, I stepped inside and kicked it shut behind me. "Girl, because you like to take forever. I told you that I wanted to catch the nurse before she left."

"Aye," my uncle groaned, stirring on the couch. "Don't be coming in here with all that loud ass talking. People in here trying to sleep."

My head snapped in his direction, and my lip curled up in disgust. I wanted to vomit at the sight of him. I couldn't understand how someone could be so damn lazy. I hated a person who wanted nothing out of life and was content with living off others. People like that made my ass itch.

I wasn't sure what he planned on doing once it was time to say our goodbyes to Grams, but no one else was going to be putting up with his bullshit.

"Is that Henry's ass?" Fatima asked, sucking her teeth.

"Yeah, that's your bum ass brother," I told her and turned my attention to my uncle, who sat mugging me. "If it ain't my grandma, I could care less about what other *people* in here trying to do. Shouldn't you be at somebody's job or something?"

"Shouldn't you be minding your own fucking business or something?" he quipped.

"Yeah, and I am," I shot back. "You might want to start figuring out what you gon' do, because you're going to need to be making other arrangements real soon."

"Little girl, who the hell do you think you are? You don't run shit. I'm *your* uncle. You better start acting like you got sense and show some respect around here."

"Hah!" I laughed in his face. "That's funny, but you heard what I said."

I turned and left him standing there cursing to my back. I wasn't playing with Henry. He could take me for a joke if he wanted to. Grams wasn't in the position to be coming to his defense anymore. His ass had to go.

Making my way to Grams' room, I peeped my head in the door to find the nurse holding a cup to Grams' mouth, helping her drink. Noticing me at the door, Grams glanced in my direction and smiled weakly.

"Hey, young woman," I said, smiling back and stepping fully into her bedroom.

Over the last couple of weeks, the room's appearance had changed drastically. Instead of the huge queen bed that once sat in the center of the room, it was now replaced with a much smaller one that hospice had provided for her. Her nightstand was covered with various pill bottles and supplies. It was almost like she had never left the hospital.

"How's she doing?" I asked the nurse, coming over to stand at Grams bedside.

"We're doing a little better with fluids today. She finished off half of her Ensure this morning," the nurse proudly declared. "Isn't that right, Mrs. Banks?"

Grams nodded as her eyes stayed glued on me. Lately it had been a struggle for her to talk, because it usually led to a fit of coughs. As the days went by, I was noticing the physical change more and more.

Her once voluptuous flesh was practically skin and bones now. Those vibrant eyes that I loved gazing into had begun to lose their light and were now sunken in. As much as I hated seeing her like this, I made sure that not a day went by that she didn't see my face. I planned on being right by her side every step of the way.

"Has she needed the pain meds any?" I questioned.

"Yes, earlier this morning, but she usually refuses them around this time. I think she just likes to be alert when she knows you guys are coming." The nurse smiled sweetly. "Her cough has gotten a bit worse, but we've been trying to sooth it as best we can. That's what's usually triggering all the other pains."

After wrapping up my conversation with the nurse, I helped her with her things to the door and returned, climbing into bed beside Grams. She was lying with her eyes closed, but I could tell that she was still awake. The low moans that she made in pain broke my heart, and all I could do was lay there and stroke her hair.

"Grams, you remember that time you found out that I had

skipped school that day in high school, trying to be fast with my lil' friends?" I laughed, continuing to play in her curly mane. "Boy, you beat my tail that day. I couldn't sit down for like a whole week. That's what I got for trying to be grown. I think Faye snitched on me, too."

Boom. Boom. Boom.

The loud banging at Grams' front door startled me and caused my face to frown. "Who in the world beating on the door like that?" I asked, getting up to see who it was.

Walking into the living room, I saw that Henry hadn't moved from his spot on the couch and rolled my eyes in his direction. I guess I was the only one that heard the door. Glancing out the window, I was confused as to why the person on the other side was there. Snatching the door open, I rudely looked them up and down, showing how displeased I was at their visit.

"What the hell are you doing at my grandmother's house and beating on the door like you don't have any sense?"

"Is that anyway to talk to your elders?"

"With all due *disrespect*, with all the bullshit you and your son put me through, you're lucky I'm only talking and not dragging your old ass up and down this sidewalk," I growled, mugging Andre's mother. "Now, I'm going to ask you one more time. What are you doing here, Gina?"

"Listen, you little heifer," she growled, quickly dropping the nice act. "I know you had something to do with my Andre getting murdered."

"What the hell? See, I know you've lost your mind now. You need to take your ass from around here with that BS," I told her, preparing to turn back around and head back inside, but she caught me by my arm, causing me to snatch away. "Don't be putting your hands on me. I'm telling you now. I don't discriminate and will whoop your old ass out here. Try me if you want to."

"You had something to do with it, or you know who did. Tell the truth," she yelled. "My baby didn't deserve that! I know this is your fault. Dre told me how you were mad about the baby and threatening to send people after him. You went too far! All of this because he didn't want you anymore!"

My head cocked to the side as I listened to the foolishness spewing from her mouth. She wasn't *that* damn dumb. I knew she couldn't have believed the crap she just said herself. We both knew her son was nothing but a habitual liar. She just needed someone to blame, and I must have been the perfect person.

"Look, I'm sorry that your bitch ass son obviously messed with the wrong person and finally got what was coming to him. My condolences to you," I insincerely said. "But I had nothing to do with whatever crap he got himself caught up in. Do me a favor, and don't bring your ass around here anymore, or you're going to end up seeing your son *real* soon."

Her mouth dropped open in shock as she stared at me with wide eyes. "Is that a threat?"

"It's whatever you want it to be, sweetheart. You have a nice day and a blessed life. Be safe out here," I told her, closing the door in her face and throwing my back against it.

I was going to kill Ash!

MARCEL

Pulling up to Shan's crib, I shut my engine off and glanced over my shoulder at Heaven, who was playing with her toys in her car seat.

"You ready to go see TeTe, mama?" I asked, smiling at her.

"TeTe," she cheerfully repeated, before starting to incoherently babble.

Getting out of the car, I moved to get Heaven from the back seat. The slamming of a door caught my attention, and everything in me was telling me not to look up. I purposefully took my time unbuckling Heaven from her seat, but evidently, I didn't take long enough. As soon as I closed the door and turned around, I cursed under my breath as I locked eyes with Mariah.

I had been doing everything in my power to avoid bumping into her. That chick had done a complete 360 on me. She had been blowing my phone up so bad that it got to the point where I just had to change my number altogether.

I was really hoping that she wouldn't even acknowledge me, seeing as though I had Heaven with me, but that was only wishful thinking. I barely took one step on the sidewalk before she was making a beeline in my direction.

"Marcel, I need to talk to you," she called out to me.

"Mariah, please don't start with this. You see I got my lil' mama right now. Gone somewhere," I said without breaking my stride.

"But it's important, Marcel. We need—"

"Mariah, I just said go on somewhere. Damn," I barked, raising my voice and causing Heaven to jump in my arms. "Daddy sorry, mama. Bye, Mariah. Take your behind back over there, and leave me alone, man."

Shan must have heard us outside because she pulled her door open and stood staring with an amused expression plastered on her face. Leaving Mariah standing there on the sidewalk and looking crazy, I marched up Shan's steps and pushed past her.

"I don't see a damn thing funny," I grumbled.

"Well, I do." Shan laughed, closing the door behind us. "I tried to tell you not to get caught up with that girl. You can just look at her and tell she a lil' off in the head."

"Be quiet, Shan," I said, trying my best not to laugh at her.

"I'm just saying, Cello. Whatever it is you're doing to these damn women, you need to stop. Don't nobody have time to be dealing with stalkers. That hoe liable to get stabbed around here."

"Watch your mouth, and quit talking crazy around my baby." I jokingly scolded her.

"Oh, whatever. You're a thousand times worse, sir," she said, reaching for Heaven. "Give me my fat mama."

I handed Heaven over and placed her diaper bag onto the coffee table. "Thanks again for watching her for me."

"Boy, gone somewhere. You know it's no problem. I've been missing my baby. She and Vana haven't had a playdate in a minute. Oh, but hold on. A little birdy told me that you and Fatima are back on good terms," she said, smirking.

"You and your nosy mama need to stay out of my business." I chuckled. "But we're straight. Nothing major." I shrugged.

"Honey, you *are* my business. Don't be trying to act brand new," she said, rolling her eyes at me. "But what the hell does nothing major mean. Are y'all back together or not?"

"Not. We're just cool, Shan. I'm not trying to go there with baby girl."

"Okay, are we talking not right now or like ever?"

"I don't know, man. But we're good, so that's all that matters. Are you done with the twenty-one questions?"

"Yeah, punk, I'm done. You better hope old girl's not still standing out there waiting on you." She snickered, walking me to the door.

Mariah's ass had better not be. I watched too many movies for her to be playing with me and I wasn't about to be dealing with the bitch from *Misery*. I didn't do crazy. She was going to mess around and catch a few hot ones fooling with me.

⊗⊗⊗

"QUIT PLAYING WITH ME, MAN. IF YOU'RE SERIOUS, WE CAN head down to the shop right now. All you gotta do is give me the word," I said, preparing to stand from the booth we were occupying.

"Who said I was playing? I've actually been thinking about it for a minute, but you weren't fooling with me. I was going to ask Ash to do it for me, but you know we don't get along at least 80 percent of the time," Fatima told me, laughing.

"And I would've gone upside your big ass head if you had let that nigga do it instead of me. What kind of mess is that?" I frowned.

"What?" she questioned innocently. "What's wrong with him tattooing me?"

"Don't nobody need to be tattooing you if it ain't me."

"But what if we had still been beefing? Then what?"

"Then you'd be out of luck and wouldn't be getting one period," I told her seriously.

"You are unbelievable." She chuckled, shaking her head at me.

"Whatever, ma. So we doing this or what?"

"Right now?"

"Hell yeah. We're not doing anything else, so why not? We're already over this way. Might as well swing by the shop."

Tossing a few bills on the table to cover our tab, I grabbed her hand and helped her up. Letting her walk ahead of me, I smiled inwardly as I trailed behind her admiring the sway of them thick hips.

The tight yoga pants that she was wearing had your boy thinking some real ungodly thoughts. I knew I said that I wasn't trying to jump back into the whole relationship thing with Fatima, but I was starting to wonder if we could maybe negotiate some benefits or something for the little "friendship" we had.

Since I had stopped fooling with Mariah, I hadn't been dealing with anyone else. I needed a break from females for a minute, but I couldn't lie and say your boy wasn't backed up.

It was proving to be almost impossible to be around Fatima and not think about bending her over and giving her the business. Fatima knew good and well what she was doing wearing all that tight shit around me. I was almost certain that she wasn't wearing any panties today either. The entire drive to the shop I had to keep my mind preoccupied, because all I could think about was turning the car around and heading straight to my crib. I had never been happier to see my shop in my life.

"I'm starting to get nervous now," Fatima said as she climbed out the passenger seat and met me on the curb.

"Don't be trying to chicken out," I said, laughing at her. "I promise you it's not that bad. I'll try to—"

"Marcel!"

Groaning, I shut my eyes and prayed that I was hearing things. Of all the times for this chick to be rolling up on me, she chose now. I was starting to think that I was going to have to handle her ass because it didn't look like she would be going away on her own.

"Marcel, you can't ignore me forever," Mariah cried out. "I really need to talk to you."

Fatima paused and looked back at Mariah and then at me. I could tell that she was wondering who the hell she was but didn't say anything.

"Actually, I can," I told Mariah. "I don't know what it's going to take for you to get it through your head that ain't shit here for you, ma. We kicked it for a minute, and the shit was cool for what it was, but that's it. You following me around and shit and popping up at my place of business like we were together or something. Cut this bullshit out, Mariah, and move the fuck on. I've been trying not to go the fuck off on yo' ass, but you're really trying my patience."

"Umm, I think I'm just going to wait for you inside," Fatima said, preparing to walk toward the door to the shop.

"Who is she?" Mariah cried. "Is she the reason why you're acting like this toward me, Marcel? Huh?"

"Mariah, leave. You're making a fool of yourself," I said, shaking my head and turning to follow behind Fatima.

"I'm pregnant, Marcel," she blurted out from behind me.

Fatima and I stopped in our tracks. Fatima's head whipped around quickly in my direction, and I could already see the moisture in her eyes that glistened under the streetlights.

Without saying a word, she turned on her heels and rushed inside, leaving me out there to deal with that nut job.

Turning my sights on Mariah, I stalked over to her so fast that I caused her to take a few of her own in the opposite direction. Roughly catching her by the arm, I pulled her toward me and grilled her hard.

"What the hell did you just say?"

"I... I'm... Well, Marcel, I—"

"Get that shit out!"

"I'm pregnant," she repeated lowly with tears streaming down her face.

Abruptly releasing her arm, I took a step away from her and ran my hands down my face. "What kind of games are you trying to play, Mariah? You think that shit is something to play with?"

"I'm not playing games, Marcel." She cried. "I've taken like three tests. I've been trying to tell you, but you've been ignoring me."

Not believing what I was hearing, I turned and headed to the door of the shop. "Go home, Mariah," I told her with my back still facing her.

"But, Marcel—"

"Go home!" I snapped. "I'll hit you up later."

I didn't stick around to hear anything else she might have had to say. I had to be the unluckiest nigga on the planet. Making my way inside the shop, I harshly exhaled and tried to prepare myself for the drama.

"Faye," I called out as I walked through the shop in search of her.

The door to Ash's studio was cracked, so I peeked my head inside to find him in the middle of a session. I was surprised that he was even here. It had been a minute since he had taken on any clients.

"What you doing here?" I asked, stepping inside.

"Bruh, don't come in here asking me questions," he quipped, stopping his gun. "I'm the one that need to be asking your dumb ass who you done went and got pregnant."

Groaning, I rolled my eyes to the ceiling.

"Yeah, nigga. I know about that shit. Faye back there on the phone with Jo cussing yo' ass out," he said, shaking his head. "You know her lil' ass already talking about messing you up, right?"

"Man, whatever. Fatima needs to stop running her damn mouth. I don't even know if the mess is true or not," I grumbled. "And keep Jo's crazy ass away from me, bruh."

"Nah, I thought that was your girl." He laughed, enjoying the shit. "You always taking her side and shit. You can handle her."

"Forget you, man." I laughed, backing out of his room and going to find Fatima.

"No. What I'm about to do is take my behind home. I'm not—"

"Man, hang up the phone," I said, startling Fatima and causing her to roll her eyes in my direction.

"I'll call you back, Jo." She sucked her teeth and slid her phone into her pocket. "You ready to take me home?"

"So that's what we're doing?"

"Yeah. It is," she replied nonchalantly. "So are you or not?"

"Man, what's up with the attitude, Fatima? Speak your mind. Don't be talking shit with Jo and then bite your tongue with me."

She could barely look me in the face without her eyes beginning to mist again. "Is she pregnant by you? That's all I want to know."

As much as I wanted to sit there and say no, I knew that I couldn't. I wasn't sure about anything right now. As crazy as I knew Mariah was, I still couldn't flat out just say that she was lying. I wasn't a sucka-ass nigga. I knew that if I was hitting it, then there would always be a possibility. Even though I was almost certain that I strapped up every time I took it there with Mariah, that shit wasn't 100 percent guaranteed.

"Faye, I can't sit here and say whether she is or isn't. I don't even know if the broad is *really* pregnant to begin with. Hell, this is my first time hearing of the shit too," I told her.

"But is there a possibility?"

From the look in her eyes, I knew that she wanted so badly for me to say no, but I couldn't.

"Yeah, Fatima. She could be." I sighed.

"Cool." She nodded. "Can you take me home now?"

"Man, don't do this, bruh," I groaned.

"I'm not doing anything, but I also don't have time for whatever the hell it is you call yourself doing," she quipped at me.

"What am I doing, Fatima? Please, explain that shit to me," I urged. "You think I would have even brought you down here if I knew her ass was going to pop up? You're sitting up here acting like I cheated on you or something."

"It's not about whether or not you cheated, Marcel!" She raised her voice. "This woman is claiming to be pregnant by you. Pregnant! Do you have any idea how stupid that makes me feel? Here I am trying to prove myself to you and regain your trust, and you're out here knocking bitches up! How would you feel if I was out here fucking off with other dudes?"

"You were! What the hell you saying?" I barked at her. "Are you forgetting why we're even at this point in the first place? If she is pregnant, that happened *after* you. I'm not the one that was fucking off while we were together. You were, so how about you think about how that shit made *me* feel. I understand you mad and in your feelings, but don't be trying to sit here and act like yo' shit don't stink."

"You know what? You're right. I messed up. This is all my fault, right? I'll take that blame. Yeah, I was letting another man trick off on me while you and I were together, but not once during *or* after you have I ever given myself to him or anyone else. But you did," she said, wiping her face. "I guess I loved your stupid ass too much to believe that we were really over, but that's been made perfectly clear tonight."

Pushing past me, she hurried and walked away without another word. I honestly didn't think me going after her would be the smartest thing to do. There was always something coming between us, and I was starting to think us being together probably wasn't in the cards. It was probably best if I just let her go. I needed to focus on figuring out all the bullshit that seemed to be falling into my lap left and right. I just couldn't seem to catch a break.

6

ASH

"Your friend is a fuck up," Jordyn fussed.

"And that's his damn business. Is the food done yet?" I asked, trying to glance over her shoulder as she stood at the stove.

"I'm serious, Ash. How is—"

"Jo, baby girl, come on. We have enough bullshit on our plate as it is. I'm not interested in taking on someone else's crap, too. Instead of worrying about somebody else's relationship, your focus needs to be on fixing *your* man a plate before I turn this damn kitchen out. I'm hungry as hell, shorty."

"Here," she snapped, rolling her eyes as she brought my food over and sat it down in front on me.

I could see that her attitude was on ten, but I wasn't about to entertain Jordyn today. I didn't understand why women did this mess. She was walking around here mad like Cello's behind had gone and had a baby on *her* or something. You'd think she was the one that had gotten cheated on with the way she was carrying on.

"Man, sit your mad ass down and come eat, Jordyn," I told

her before stuffing a forkful of mashed potatoes in my mouth. "If you ask me, both of y'all blowing the shit out of proportion and only making a bad situation worse."

"Yeah, of course, *you* would think that."

"Yeah, because I seem to be the only one thinking with some sense," I retorted. "Look, I'm not saying the situation isn't kind of messed up, because it is, but what exactly did he do wrong? Were they together or even speaking to each other when Cello was bussin' down old girl?"

Rolling her eyes in my direction, she sucked her teeth. "Do you have to say it like that?"

"Shorty, that was the PG version." I shrugged. "Were they or weren't they?"

"No, but—"

"Then that's all that matters. This mess right here ain't nothing but a test to see whether they need to be together in the first place. If this too much for her, then she needs to walk away. Simple."

"It's not simple, because she loves his punk ass."

"Then *her* punk ass needs to suck the shit up and put on her big girl panties. Y'all women make stuff so difficult."

"Whatever. Difficult my behind." She snorted and glanced down at my already half-empty plate. "Boy, slow down. You're eating like it's going somewhere."

"It might not be, but I am."

"And where might that be?" she questioned, leaning back and folding her arms across her chest. "I thought you were chilling with me for the rest of the night."

"Some shit came up. I got to make a quick run, but I shouldn't be gone for too long," I advised her. "Call your girl, and tell her to come through until I get back. Y'all can finish doggin' my boy like he ain't shit."

"That's because he ain't." She laughed. "But I might just go over there with her. I'm sure she's probably not going to feel like driving all the way out here."

"Just make sure you call me on your way out," I told her, glancing down at my ringing phone.

"So you're still ignoring his calls?" Jordyn asked, glancing down at the name that flashed across the screen. "Ash, he's your brother. Maybe you should just hear what he has to say."

"Drop it, Jordyn." I spoke with my jaw tightly clenched. I stood from my seat and rounded the table to place a kiss on her forehead. "I'm about to dip. Thanks for dinner, ma."

❄️

"AND YOU KNOW FOR SURE THAT'S WHERE HE'S BEEN HIDING out at?" I asked one of my men as they gave me the rundown of the info they'd found on Brent.

"Yeah, my boy say that yo' bro has been up that way for a minute, laying low."

I was tired of playing the little cat and mouse game with him, and I was ready to put an end to this shit tonight. Brent couldn't dodge me forever, and he was lucky to have avoided me for so long, but his time *and* my patience had run out a long time ago.

"How you want to handle this, boss?" one of my other soldiers asked.

"I don't want anyone making any moves without my say. I don't care if you're standing right in front of that lil' nigga. Stand down until I give the word," I ordered. "That's still my fucking brother, and I'll body any one of you motherfuckers if you even harm a hair on that pussy's head. Understood?"

I glanced around to make sure that everyone was clear on their orders. I didn't need a big team to get at Brent, but I knew that I couldn't be everywhere at once. Brent's little ass was known for getting ghost in a second. The more eyes on him the better.

"I guess we're headed to Charlotte. Let's roll," I told my men.

"Yo, Ash!"

Groaning, I cut my eyes toward the entrance. "I'm busy. What?"

"Bro, don't *what* me," Dylan quipped. "Morgan and I have been blowing your damn phone up. Why haven't you been answering for us?"

"Boy, who the fuck you think you talking to?" I asked, turning to face Dylan.

"You, man," he replied, standing his ground. "Ash, you know this isn't even us. You been acting bogus as fuck. I know you pissed about everything with B, but you taking it out on all of us."

"Dylan, I don't have time for this."

"Since when don't you have time for *me*, Ashley? Your baby brother?"

"Man, don't be trying to use that shit." I waved him off. "That brother shit obviously don't mean shit anymore."

Pulling my vibrating phone from my pocket, I saw that it was Jordyn and knew that she must have been calling to let me know that she had left my house already and was heading to Fatima's. Ignoring Dylan, I answered the call.

"You left yet, baby?"

"Ash! They—"

Hearing the panic and distress in Jordyn's voice caused me to immediately switch into high alert.

"Jordyn?"

There was shuffling on the line, and voices could be heard in the distance before the line went silent. Pulling the phone from my ear, I saw that the call was still connected.

"Jo, you there?" I asked, rushing to the table covered in guns and grabbing the first thing I could get my hands on. "Jordyn—"

"This ain't Jordyn, motherfucker." A deep, muffled voice came on the line.

"Yo, who the fuck is this? I swear to God if you hurt her, I'm—"

"Shut the hell up!" they barked. "You're in no position to be making threats."

My chest heaved up and down as I attempted to calm myself. "Who is this, and what the hell do you want?"

You good? Dylan mouthed, coming to stand closer to me.

I ignored him as I tried to focus on the caller's voice. It was hard to really decipher what they were saying, because they were trying their best to keep their voice disguised.

"If you want your bitch back alive, you'd do what the fuck I say," they demanded.

My frustration was growing by the second, so I didn't bother to respond and just waited for their instructions.

"I want five million cash by midnight tonight. You—"

"Five million? Nigga, do you know what time it is? You expect me to get that shit to you in two hours?" I snapped at him.

"I don't give a fuck what time it is," they barked. "You got it. I know that's not even putting a dent in your pockets, so make it happen. Be waiting for my call. Oh, and bring that bitch with you."

"What bitch?" I asked, having an idea of who they were referring to.

Their request only confirmed my suspensions. It blew my mind how much hatred one person could have for me. I never would have thought that he'd take things *this* far.

"Don't play dumb with me. You know *exactly* what bitch I'm talking about. Don't have her there, and your girl dies. I'm not too fond of her smart-mouthed ass anyway, so try me if you think I'm playing," he advised. "I don't want any slick shit from you either. Make sure you come alone."

"How you expect me to come alone if you just said bring a bitch with me?" I smartly questioned.

"Ahh!" I could hear Jordyn scream in the background.

"Keep playing with me, and this hoe won't make it. Get my fucking money, and you better answer when I call," he growled right before disconnecting the call.

I wanted so badly to chuck the damn phone clear across the room, but I refrained myself. I needed it so that they could reach me with the meetup location.

"Ash, what the hell was that about?" Dylan asked, still standing in front of me waiting for answers.

"Not now, Dylan. Damn!" I snapped, pacing back and forth.

"What's the move?" one of my men asked.

"He's not in Charlotte. He's here," I informed my men.

"Here? You sure? I mean, my boy said—"

"I don't give a damn what your boy said." My voice thundered throughout the warehouse. "That motherfucker's here, and he has my lady!"

"Just tell us what you need for us to do." They all stood around waiting for my instructions.

"Nothing," I told them. "I'm handling this shit alone."

"Alone? But boss—"

"You heard what I said! All I need for you niggas to do is what you been doing. I want eyes on all my traps, and make sure all my shit is moving as it should be."

I locked eyes with everyone in the room to be sure that they understood their orders. I was sure the majority of them weren't feeling me going on the mission solo, and honestly, neither was I. As much as my gut was telling me that I was about to make a huge mistake, I had to go through with it. Jordyn's life depended on it.

"Aye, Ash! Wait up, man," Dylan called out as he jogged behind me, trying to catch me as I made my way to my car.

"I don't have time for this shit, Dylan."

"Bro, I don't care what you have time for. I'm not about to let you do this shit alone. I'm going with you, Ash."

"No the hell you're not. Go home, Dylan," I said, opening my car door.

"Ash, you need me—"

"Go home! I don't need you to do anything other than get the hell out my face," I barked, slamming my door shut and throwing my car into gear.

Instead of wasting time going back and forth with Dylan, I needed to get to my crib so that I could get the damn money together and get Misty's ass.

Yes, I still had the bitch locked up in my basement. I meant it when I said that she was going to be staying there until she had that damn baby. She must have been doing some heavy praying down there because things seemed to be looking up for her a little.

If it had not been for them taking my lady, I wouldn't have even considered turning Misty over. However, my love for Jordyn and need for her to be safe outweighed anything else.

"Get up," I barked, bursting through the cellar door and flicking the light on.

"Huh?" Misty groaned, stirring awake. "Is the doctor here?"

"Aye, don't be asking me any damn questions. Just get your ass up. We got somewhere to be."

I saw the fear in her eyes, and I was sure she was thinking that it would be the day that I finally put her out of her misery and ended her pathetic life. Being the asshole that I was, I didn't plan on telling her otherwise. Who knew? Maybe I would still get the opportunity to put a bullet in her ass.

❧

SPARKING UP MY BLUNT, I RECLINED MY SEAT SOME AND rested my head back. I still had no clue where I was supposed to be meeting those motherfuckers, and it was already a quarter to midnight. Something was telling me that they were going to pull some bullshit like that.

I was so ready for the shit to be over with. My only concern at that point was getting Jordyn out unharmed. If it took for me to lose my life in the process to make that happen then so be it. I was tired. It seemed like it was always going to be something.

After sitting on the side of the road for what felt like hours, my phone chimed in my lap, signaling an incoming text. Quickly checking its contents, I found a message from an unknown number with an address included.

The address was all too familiar, and I knew exactly where we were meeting—my warehouse. I had a few spread out all over the city, and that one in particular was one that we had been stopped using and only used it for storage. If it wasn't clear to me before who was behind things, it damn sure was now.

Throwing my car into gear, I pulled back onto the dark road and headed in the warehouse's direction. I had no clue what was going to be waiting for me once I got there, but there was still not an ounce of fear in my body. I wouldn't dare give those motherfuckers the satisfaction.

The closer I got to my destination, the more my anxiety grew. The feeling in my gut intensified as it tried to warn me of the dangers ahead. Everything in me screamed that I was walking straight into a setup, but I couldn't turn back, not when Jordyn's life depended on me.

Pulling onto the dirt road that would lead me back to the warehouse, I cut the lights to my car and slowly crept up to the building. Taking a quick survey of my surroundings, nothing seemed out of place, but there was still this eerie feeling that settled around me.

My phone rang in my lap, and I groaned after seeing that it was Morgan. It was definitely the wrong time. I didn't have time to hear his mouth. Turning my phone completely off, I tossed it in the backseat and took a deep breath before stepping out of the car.

"Showtime."

۞

STEPPING INSIDE THE DANK WAREHOUSE, I GRIPPED MISTY'S arm as I pulled her frame beside me with one hand while gripping the strap of the duffle bag with the other. I was already on high alert and anticipating shit popping off at any second. We had barely taken two steps inside when the hairs of the back of my neck rose.

Even though the place was eerily quiet and seemed to be empty, we weren't alone. I could sense someone somewhere else in the room but wasn't able to locate them because of how dark it was. Dropping Misty's arm and removing my gun from my waist, I was prepared for whatever.

Before I could take another step, something moving in my peripheral caught my eyes. Just as I was about to raise my gun in that direction, gunshots rang out, causing me to push Misty to the ground.

Pfft. Pfft.

My body instinctively ducked as a bullet whizzed right

above my head. Whoever was behind the trigger was trying to take my shit clean off. Ducking behind one of the concrete pillars, I crouched down and extended my arm out, returning fire in the direction the bullets were coming from.

"Argh!" I heard someone grunt.

That motivated me to keep shooting. It was still unclear exactly how many I was up against, but it didn't make me any difference. I was determined to make it out of there—with Jordyn.

"Shit," I mumbled after feeling a burning sensation shoot through my shoulder.

Wincing in pain, my steps faltered slightly at the feeling of another bullet ripping through my flesh. It might not have been able to stop me, but it was damn sure was enough to slow me down. I cursed under my breath after glancing down and seeing bright crimson begin to paint the side of my shirt, causing it to cling to my skin.

"Ash!" I could hear Jordyn's fearful cry sound off.

My head whipped in the direction of Jordyn's voice, but I was met with the butt of a gun, dazing me momentarily. I didn't plan on going down without a fight. Staggering a little, I regained my footing and was about raise my gun in their direction.

"I wouldn't do that if I were you," a muffled voice taunted.

My entire body stalled at the sight of a gun being pressed firmly against the side of Jordyn's head as she stood there visibly petrified. My jaw clenched after watching her captor pull her closer to him by her hair. The shadows casting over their face concealed their identity, but it didn't take a rocket scientist for me to figure out who the person was.

"Put your gun down, or I'll drop this bitch right now!"

The wheels began to turn in my head as I tried to quickly think of a plan that wouldn't end with both of us getting killed.

"Try some slick shit if you want to," they called out to me and turned to Jordyn. "That nigga obviously can't love you too much if he's willing to risk your life like this."

Not seeing any other option, I did as they instructed and slowly lowered myself, placing my gun beside me. Before I could return to a standing position, I was struck across the back of the head again.

"Nah. Stay yo' ass down there."

"My nigga, you know I'm killing you once this is all over, right?" I said over my shoulder.

"You actually think you're about to make it out of here?"

The laughter from the both of them caused a fire to ignite within me.

"Cut the bullshit, Brent," I barked, tired of the charades and games. "You hiding in the shadows like a lil' bitch. Bruh, I'm not stupid, so we can cut it with all this mystery bullshit. Do what you got to do, but make that shit quick because you've already wasted enough of my damn time."

I wasn't in the best position to be talking shit, but I also wasn't in the position to be sitting here playing around with those motherfuckers. They could keep the dramatics. I was starting to get a little lightheaded, and there was no telling how much blood I had lost from the two gunshot wounds and the blows I'd taken to the head.

Brent chuckled as he stepped into the dim light, revealing his face. It still amazed me just how much hatred he held for me, and I had no clue where it came from or when it started.

"See, that's your problem right there. You always think you're running shit." Brent menacingly chuckled. "I would have thought you'd learned by now."

"B, you of all people should know I'm not for all the talking. All I want to know is why. What the hell have I done to you to make you hate me so much?"

"Nigga, you know exactly what you did. Hell, what you *still* do," he quipped. "Everything is always about *Ash* and what *Ash* says. You always have to control shit. Always have to be the boss of shit. D and Morg might be okay with it, but I ain't your lil' bitch that's just gon' do whatever the hell you say. You—"

"Well, you sure as hell do sound like a lil' bitch right now. You must have gotten that shit from your daddy." I cut him off, shaking my head. "You righteously did all this out of jealousy, bruh? Really? What type of sucka shit is that? What the fuck do you have to be jealous of! You can't even give me a real reason. You sitting here butt hurt because your young, dumb ass ain't in charge, but Morg and I bust our asses out here just to make sure that you and D are straight!" My voice boomed.

"Nigga, I ain't never asked you or Morg for a damn thing," he barked back. "Y'all don't deserve this shit! You don't even want it! You love to throw shots at Pops, but without him, you wouldn't be shit!"

"Bruh, fuck you *and* your bitch-ass daddy. I mean that from the bottom of my heart," I said coolly. "Now, I'm done talking. Either you're going to quit being a pussy and use that gun in your hands, or quit wasting my time. This shit is pathetic and petty as hell."

"Oh, you think I won't?" he asked.

"I *think* I don't care either way. I'm over this whole thing." I shrugged. "I brought the money like you asked and even that snake ass bitch. Granted, she's laid out over there dead as a doorknob, but that's on you. Probably shouldn't have come in this bitch like you were Rambo or some damn body. All I know is I kept up my end. If you gon' bust a move, then do it, but let Jordyn go first."

A sinister smile crossed his face as he looked Jordyn up and down. "Oh, I'm going to let her go, but not before I get me a sample of that pussy. She looks like she's carrying some fire. I'll even be nice enough to let you watch. That's the least I can do since this will be the last time you'll be seeing her or anyone else for that matter."

I watched as Jordyn's eyes widened at his words, and she struggled in his grip. The mere mention of him even *thinking* to touch her sent me into a rage. Before I could move from where I was still positioned on my knees, a shot rang out. Seconds later, the body that was once standing behind me with the gun pressed to my head dropped to the ground behind me.

"Ahhh!"

My eyes frantically shot back in Jordyn's direction, and my teeth gritted. I watched Brent snatch Jordyn in front of him, using her as a shield.

"I should have known your lying ass didn't come alone!" Brent yelled.

"Put the gun down, Brent!"

Brent's eyes immediately went to our new guest, but mine never left Jordyn. I tried to communicate with her as best as I could with my eyes.

"Ash," she quietly murmured.

"Everything's going to be okay, baby. I promise." I tried to sooth her.

"Bitch, shut up! Everything's not going to be okay," Brent barked, aiming his gun at me.

"Brent! I said put that shit down!"

"Get the hell out of here, Dylan! This ain't got nothing to do with you," Brent growled in Dylan's direction with his eyes and gun still trained on me.

Dylan moved further into the warehouse and close enough for us all to see him. I should have known that his hard-headed behind wasn't going to listen to me, but for once, I was glad he hadn't.

"What the hell you mean this don't have anything to do

with me? We're brothers! Drop the damn gun, B!" Dylan yelled, aiming at Brent.

Brent's eyes grew wide in shock before it was quickly replaced by anger. "Really, D? You gon' turn on me for *this* motherfucker? That's how we doing it now, Dylan?"

"Yo, B. You're tripping. Ain't nobody turning on you, but you're stupid if you think I'm about to sit here and let you kill my fucking brother—our brother!"

"What about me! I'm your brother too! When it comes to this motherfucker, I guess it's fuck me, though, huh?" He nodded. "Well fuck you, Ash, and his hoe. As far as I'm concerned, we can all go tonight. I'm ready. Are you? Let's see if you're as quick with that stick as you think you are, lil' nigga."

"Ashley!" Jordyn screamed.

"Brent, don't do this!" Dylan yelled at the same time as her. *Pow! Pow!*

7

JORDYN

Still balled in a fetal position, my body violently shook as I waited for my ears to stop ringing from the gunshots that had just rang out. I was almost afraid to open my eyes, scared of the scene that would be waiting on me. The seconds that passed felt like hours as the warehouse fell into an eerie silence.

"Fuck! No! No, man!"

At the sound of Dylan's panicking voice, my eyes shot open and quickly darted around my surrounded. After noticing blood on the side of my shirt, I reflexively began to inspect myself for injuries. Relief washed over me after realizing that the fluids didn't belong to me. However, that relief was short lived after catching sight of Ash bent over in obvious pain a few yards in front of me.

"No, Jordyn," Ash said, shaking his head and stopping me before I could move in his direction.

My eyes were trained on him as he grimaced in pain and struggled to walk in my direction, but his eyes weren't on me.

"Ash, man, I didn't—" Dylan started, but Ash cut him off before he could finish.

"Take Jordyn, and get out of here, Dylan," Ash instructed without looking at him.

Ash didn't stop moving until he was directly in front of Brent and dropped down to his knees. His fingers moved to Brent's neck to check for a pulse, but we all already knew that there wasn't one. Brent's lifeless eyes were cast up at the ceiling as his mouth hung open, and blood seeped from between his lips.

"Man, no. What about you, Ash?" Dylan questioned. "You're bleeding all over the place. We need to get you to Doc."

"Don't worry about me. Just do what I said!"

"Ashley, baby, pleas—"

"Go!"

My body involuntary jumped as his harsh command boomed throughout the warehouse. Hot tears were cascading down my face as I choked on the cries that fought to be released. I could feel my heart literally trying to escape my chest as I struggled to breath. It felt as if the walls were closing in around me as I tried to draw breath into my burning lungs.

"Come on, Jordyn. We have to go."

I felt Dylan's arms wrap around me as he tried to get me to move. Snatching away, I refused to walk away and abandon Ash like that. There was no way they could make me.

"I'm not leaving him!" I yelled defiantly. "We—"

Obviously tired of tussling and going back and forth with me, Dylan snatched me up with strength that I didn't realize he possessed and roughly threw me over his shoulder. My heart broke with each step we took from where Ash sat hovering above his brother's lifeless body.

"Dylan, we can't just leave him like this! Please," I begged while he continued to ignore me.

I cringed as I caught a glimpse of Misty's bloody frame sprawled across the cold concrete right before we stepped outside into the humid night air. We didn't stop moving until we came to a car, which I assumed belonged to Dylan, and he opened the door to toss me into the backseat. My initial reaction was to go straight for the door, only to discover that the child lock was on.

"Let me out! What kind of brother are you? How can you just leave him!" I screamed, kicking against the driver seat's headrest as he got inside and started the car. "I am not—"

"Shut the fuck up, and sit back!" Dylan yelled, slamming his fists into the steering wheel as his chest heaved up and down.

Huffing, my mouth clamped shut as I slammed my back against the seat. From where I was sitting, I could see that I wasn't the only one messed up about this. Tears drenched Dylan's face as he stared straight ahead at the road. Aside from the constant sniffles I just couldn't seem to control, the car was silent.

After what felt like forever, we pulled into a familiar driveway, and I realized that we were at Morgan's place. Barely throwing the car in park, Dylan threw his door open and mine followed. He had made it to the front door before I could blink. Not knowing what else to do, I slowly got out and forced my shivering body to move, making my way up the walkway to the porch.

"Where the hell have you been, D?" Morgan barked after snatching his door open. "I've been blowing your phone up for the past hour and—Wait. Is that blood? What the hell, Dylan? What the fuck happened?"

Morgan took him by the shoulders so that he could examine him, but Dylan pulled away.

"It's not mine." Dylan barely managed to get that out through his tears and rapid breathing.

"Then whose is it?" Morgan stopped, and his eyes traveled over to where I stood behind Dylan, seemingly noticing me for the first time. "Jordyn? What are you doing here? What the hell is going on? Dylan, you better start talking now! Where is Ash?"

"Brent, man." Dylan struggled to speak, viscously shaking his head. He was probably trying to rid himself of the visual that must have been replaying in his head.

"Brent?" he stammered with a raised brow, looking back and forth between the two of us. "Wha—Where... What about Brent? Where's Ash?"

An ugly cry escaped from deep within my gut as my body violently shook.

"One of y'all better start telling me something! Where the hell are Ashley and Brent?" He yelled.

"There at 19th Street," Dylan answered, shaking his head. "Morgan, B's gone. He's gone, man. I—"

Before Dylan could finish his sentence, Morgan had already snatched up his keys and was halfway to his car. Dylan rushed to follow behind him, but Morgan stopped him.

"Stay here with Jordyn, D," he instructed him.

"But, Morg—"

"Dylan, I need you to stay with her. I'll handle this shit," Morgan assured him. "Just don't leave Jordyn."

☙❧

DYLAN HAD BEEN PACING BACK AND FORTH IN FRONT OF ME since Morgan walked out of the door almost two hours ago.

Neither of us spoke a word to each other. I guess we were both too consumed in our own thoughts. Flashbacks of what had taken place tonight kept replaying in my head, making it damn near impossible to think of anything else.

As much as I tried to convince myself that everything was going to be okay, I knew deep down that probably was the furthest thing from the truth. I wasn't even sure whether Ash was okay. With all the blood that he seemed to have lost, I wasn't so confident that he would be.

Dylan abruptly stopped pacing at the same time my head snapped up after hearing the front door slam. My heartrate sped up, anticipating Ash rounding the corner. Before either of us could move, Marcel was shooting around the corner with concern lacing his face. He was the last person I was expecting to be coming through the door. Jumping to my feet, I rushed to him and threw myself into his arms.

"Marcel," I barely managed through my tears.

"Jo, calm down, baby girl." He attempted to sooth me. "Man, what the hell is going on? Morgan called me and just told me I needed to get here. I've been calling Ash, and he's not answering. And Jo, Faye's been blowing you up since last night—Wait."

After noticing the blood on my clothes, I could tell he became alarmed. "It's not mine," I said quietly. "It's Brent's."

"Tell me what happened, Jordyn," he demanded impatiently.

"I was supposed to be going to meet Faye, and some niggas grabbed me. It all happened so fast, Cel. They shot him!"

Marcel's body tensed, and he quickly pushed me away from him. "Shot who?" he asked frantically.

"Ash. He was going to kill him if Dylan hadn't shown up when he did. They shot him like—"

"Don't tell me that shit!" he snapped, catching me off guard. "Don't tell me that, Jordyn. Where is Ash? He's okay, right?"

Marcel's eyes shot over to Dylan, and I looked on as they silently communicated with each other.

"Morg has him. They're at Doc's. I'm waiting to hear back," Dylan mumbled, dropping his head. "I swear I didn't want to leave him there, man, but he made me. I had to get her out of there."

"It's okay, D. Chill. You know how Ash is, and I'm sure he

had his reasons for doing it," Marcel told him, trying to calm Dylan down. "Look, I'm going to run Jo home, and I'll swoop back by here once I get her settled. You gon' be good?"

"Yeah, man." Dylan sighed with uncertainty.

I looked back at Dylan with sad eyes as Marcel and I headed for the door. After everything that had taken place, I didn't think it was the smartest idea for him to be left alone. I might not have known Dylan all that well, and he might have appeared tough on the exterior, but having to kill your brother would be enough to break anyone.

"He'll be okay, Jo," Marcel assured me after noticing me staring at Dylan. "Let's get you home."

⚜

"ARE YOU SURE YOU'RE OKAY WITH BEING THERE BY yourself? You know I don't mind staying there with you, Jo," Fatima told me. "I mean, at least until Ash gets back."

"That's okay, Faye. I'm good," I assured her. "I need this minute to myself anyways. It's been so much going on. I don't know whether I'm coming or going."

"I know, Jordyn, but after finding out what happened, I don't know if I'm comfortable with you being there alone."

"There's nothing to be worried about. Brent's out of the picture now, so as far as I know, there's not much of a threat anymore."

I knew it wasn't right to wish death on anyone, but I was glad that Brent got what was coming to him. It was unfortunate that it was Ash's little brother that we were talking about, but at the end of the day, I'd rather it be him than Ash. Brent knew exactly what he was getting himself into and where his actions would lead him. He chose his fate.

"I bet his other little brother is taking this so hard," she said, referring to Dylan. "I know this has to be messing with him. I can't even imagine having to do something like that, Jo. I mean, his own brother? Damn."

"I know." I sighed. "It's different when you're actually there in the situation. If your own brother is telling you that he's ready to kill all of y'all, including himself, what else are you supposed to do? I just—"

"I would appreciate it if you wouldn't be telling my family's business to the fucking world."

The sudden intrusion of Ash's deep baritone startled me, almost causing my phone to slip from my grasp. My eyes shot over to him, and I was stunned into silence. The entire warehouse ordeal had gone down six days ago. I knew because I had been counting, and this was my first time laying eyes on Ash. Even though Morgan had promised that Ash was okay, I wasn't taking anyone's word but my own. I needed to see Ashley for myself.

Forgetting that Fatima was still on the phone, I dropped it and almost tripped over my feet trying to get to him. My hands ran amuck over him as I checked his wounds. tears sprang to my eyes after discovering the numerous bandages covering his body.

"Oh my God, baby," I choked out, throwing my arms around his neck and crying into his chest. "Ash, I was sooo scared. I didn't think you were coming back to me. Why didn't you call me, Ashley? You had me losing my mind in this house."

His arms carefully rose to remove my arms from around his neck, and I could tell that he wasn't completely healed by the way his face grimaced in discomfort.

"I'm good, but damn. You throwing yourself all on me like you forgot a nigga got shot," he grumbled.

My head snapped back at his words and the harshness in his tone. "Nah, I haven't forgotten. That's why I've been worried about your ass. Since you're so good, you mind telling me why I haven't heard from you? I've literally spoken with everyone *but* you, Ashley. Why is that?"

He shrugged as he began to make his way through the house and toward the kitchen. "I needed time to myself."

"Okay? That's still not telling me why you couldn't at least pick up the phone and call. Hell, even if it was just a quick 'hey, just letting you know I'm still alive' call."

"But you *knew* I was," he stated nonchalantly. "I sent Morg by here."

"I ain't *know* shit. Morgan is not you," I quipped. "Did you really think that made me feel any better just because you sent your brother over? One of your *brothers* is the reason for all of this shit to begin with!"

"Look, man, I'm not in the mood for this right now. I'm tired as fuck and still hurting like a motherfucker. I needed to clear my head, so that's what I did. If I would have known I was going to come back to this, I probably would have stayed away a little longer."

"You know what?" I chuckled, feeling myself getting pissed off. "You didn't have to stay away at all. This is *your* house. I can easily leave with no problem, and you can have all the time to yourself that you need."

"See, there you go about to blow shit out of proportion. Now you talking about leaving. What's wrong with me needing to be alone, Jordyn?"

"Oh, there's absolutely nothing wrong with you being alone. The problem is that you act like you don't know how to communicate that to me. I'm your woman. Instead of just going ghost and popping back up when you're good and ready, at least have the decency to give me a heads up. We're not talking about you just being mad at me and not talking to me for a couple of days. You were shot, Ashley! Fucking shot! I was *there* in case you forgot. I had to sit there and *watch* you damn near bleed to death in front of me, *and* you made me leave you there!"

"I don't need you to remind me. This shit *here* is reminder enough," he barked, lifting his shirt.

"Yeah, a reminder for me that I could have lost you, Ashley. You're not the only one that went through some traumatic shit that night. All I'm trying to do is get you to understand why I wanted to be there for you—why I *needed* to be there—but you chose to shut me out like you always do instead," I said, shaking my head. "What do you need me for, Ash? Why am I here?"

"Yo, are we really doing *this* now?"

"You know what? We're not," I told him. "I really am glad that you're okay and I got to see for myself. Whenever you *are* ready to do this, let me know. Until then, I'll get out of your way."

I turned, looking around the room for where I had discarded my keys earlier so that I could leave. I wasn't in the habit of staying where I wasn't wanted or intruding on anyone's space.

"Jordyn," Ash called, blowing out a frustrated breath after I didn't answer and refused to look at him.

After not being able to locate the keys, I retraced my steps and moved toward the living room.

"Jordyn, where you going?" he called out again. "I'm not in the condition to be chasing behind you, but don't think I won't. Bring your butt here, man."

"You're not about to be chasing anyone," I instructed. "Go sit down somewhere before you bust your stitches open. I'm almost sure you haven't healed."

"Fuck these stitches. Come here, Jordyn," he said, catching up to me and pulling me to him by the arm.

I allowed him to lead me over to the sofa and hesitantly

took a seat beside him. He ran his hands down his face before speaking again.

"You're right, Jo. It was messed up for me to shut you out like that, but that's how I deal. I'm not used to this shit, ma. I'm used to dipping out and saying fuck everybody until I'm in a good space. Everyone knows how I am. It's just how I operate."

"What if that doesn't work for me? What if that's not how I operate? You can't do that and expect me to be okay. I—"

"I know that, Jo, but I'm trying, baby. I promise I am. This shit is just hard," he said, looking into my eyes. "Ma, I ain't never had a chick ride for me as hard as you do and that shit it foreign to me. I'm righteously still trying to get used to having someone who actually gives a damn about *me* and my well-being. You asked me why you're here, and it's because I don't know what I would do without your lil' ass. You keep me level, baby girl. I know it may not seem like it, and I probably spaz on you more often than not, but you take that shit and put me in my place. I need that. You don't let me get away with shit."

He shook his head and released a low chuckle. "Even with three damn bullets in my ass, you still in here chewing me out and ready to beat my ass."

"Because you were talking to me like you were crazy." I pouted.

"And I apologize for that," he said, kissing my forehead. "I just got mad hearing you talking to Fatima, and I snapped. I was still out of line for how I came at you, though. I'm sorry for dipping out on you too. That was fucked up, and I knew it, but I was thinking about myself."

"See what we're doing?"

"What?" he asked in confusion.

"Communicating. You're actually talking to me," I acknowl-edged. "That's all I ever asked of you was for you to keep it one hundred with me... for you to just express yourself to me, and tell me what's going on. I don't like being left in the dark. Next time, just talk to me. If you want to be alone, cool. Just *tell* me that. Is that too much to ask?"

"Not at all, baby. Just be patient with a brother. I'm not with you trying to leave me and shit. My past relationships were garbage, so all this mess is new to me, man. I know that's not an excuse, but just bear with me, Jo. You gon' have to teach me how to do this thing the right way."

"I don't know about all that." I laughed. "My track record's not so great either."

"Well, I guess we'll just have to learn together, baby girl."

8

MARCEL

Reclining back against the driver's seat, I sat in my car, trying to decide on whether I really wanted to get out. I had been avoiding it for the longest, but it was time for that to stop. Regardless of how messed up I felt the situation was, I had to man up and handle my business.

Cutting my engine, I stepped out the car and glanced across the street at Mariah's townhouse. Lowkey, I was hoping that she wouldn't be home, but the two cars parked in her driveway shot those dreams down quick. I guess that was a good thing because I couldn't keep putting this off.

It had been a little over a week since Mariah popped up at the shop and dropped the news of her possibly carrying my child on me. The shock of it all still hadn't worn off.

Taking a deep breath, I lifted my fist to the door and tapped firmly against it a few times. Movement could be heard coming from the other side, but after a few minutes of waiting, I was starting to grow impatient.

"Aye, Mariah. Open the door, man," I called out, knocking

again. "I'm not about to be standing out here knocking all day when I know your behind is in there."

"What do you want, Marcel?" Mariah asked without bothering to open the door.

"Yo, really, ma? Man, I know you better open this door. You got me standing out here on your porch talking to you through the door like some sucka ass nigga. Quit playing with me," I quipped, trying my best not to *really* go off like I wanted to.

Mariah lived in a pretty nice community, and I was almost positive these bourgeois folks around here wouldn't hesitate to call the police on my ass if it even looked like I wanted to start something. I didn't need or want those problems.

I could hear her fumbling with the locks on the other side of the door before it was slightly pulled open, and her head appeared through the crack. My face twisted into a frown as she used the door to shield the rest of her body from my view.

"Bruh, what the hell are you doing?" I questioned.

"I'm busy. What are you doing here, Marcel?" she had the audacity to ask me.

"Mariah, don't ask me no silly shit like that. You know exactly what I'm doing here. Now, let me in, so we can talk."

"Now is not a good time. If you would have called first instead of just coming over unannounced, you would know that. I have a guest, and this can wait."

"No, the hell it can't, especially not after you brought your ass down to my business with your bullshit. Your guest is what can wait, so tell them they'll have to come back another time."

"When I tried to talk to you about my 'bullshit,' as you like to refer to it as, you didn't want to hear me out and talk to me, so now you—Hey, what are you doing?" she shrieked as I pushed past her and invited myself inside her house.

Mariah must have had me confused with one of those square ass corporate dudes that she was used to messing with because she was coming at me all types of wrong. I wasn't about to do that back and forth BS with her. She was already starting to be the baby mama from hell, and I wasn't even sure if she was my baby mama yet.

"Marcel, you need to leave now," she nervously said, glancing behind me.

"I'm not going no damn where until I get some answers," I told her, reaching into my pocket and tossing the plastic drug store bag her way. "Go handle that."

"What is this?" she stuttered.

"What does it look like?" I mocked her. "Quit playing, ma, and let's get this over with. I don't want to be here any more than you want me to be."

"Why would I need to take a pregnancy test? I already told you that I was. That should be good enough. I'm not a liar, Marcel," she quipped.

"Good for you, but I'm also not stupid. If you're not lying, then taking it shouldn't be an issue," I told her, shrugging.

"I'm not taking that test," she declared, raising her voice slightly. "You should—"

"Is everything okay, sweetheart?"

We both turned at the same time as some lame ass Poindexter entered the living room. He stopped next to her, tossing his arm possessively around her shoulder. His eyes scanned over me as he sized me up. Chuckling, I slid both my hands into my pockets in an attempt to keep myself from snatching his *and* her behind up. I saw why she was so anxious to get my up out of here.

"Umm. Yes, dear. Could you give me a minute with my friend? He was just leaving," she said, giving me a look, and he moved toward me.

I hope she didn't actually believe I was about to go along with that. I didn't know what kind of games Mariah called herself trying to play, but she was going to be playing them hoes by herself.

"Actually, I wasn't," I declared, walking past them to make myself comfortable on her sofa. "Not until we handle what I came here for."

"And what exactly did you come here for?" old lame ass had the nerve to ask me. "If my woman says that it's time for you to leave, then that's just that. We don't want any problems, so if you could leave peacefully, that would be greatly appreciated."

"*If you could leave peacefully, that would be greatly appreciated,*" I childishly mocked him. "Bruh, shut yo' ass up. I don't believe I was even talking to you. Gon' somewhere and mind your business. On second thought, this just *might* be your business too, especially since you're claiming her ass as yours. Might you be claiming that baby too?"

"Marcel," Mariah called out in a pleading tone.

"What business is it to you?" he asked, looking back between us.

"Well, your girl here seems to believe that there child belongs to your boy. At least that's what she's telling me." I folded my arms across my chest and stared hard at Mariah, who looked as if she was seconds away from pissing herself.

"What!"

His head whipped in her direction so fast that I was surprised it didn't snap. Before he could even get another word out, she had already started with the waterworks.

"Don't start with the tears, Mariah. Who is this man, and what the hell is he talking about? You need to be explaining yourself now," he demanded.

"It's not what you think, Gerald." She cried hysterically. "It's all just a misunderstanding."

"I don't think I misunderstood you showing up at my place of business while I was with my woman, claiming to be carrying my seed," I insisted. "You were pretty clear with what you meant if you ask me."

"Can you just go!" Mariah yelled at me.

"No, I think he should stay," her dude asserted. "You owe us both some answers, Mariah. Is that my child you're carrying or his?"

"Hell, I'm still trying to figure out if there's really even a baby in the first place," I said, shrugging.

"Oh, there's definitely a baby. I went with her this morning for her first appointment."

"So what was your purpose of pulling that little stunt if you sitting here playing house with this man? Why even bring this bullshit to me?"

"Because it's not fair that you can so easily give what I've been practically begging you for to that bitch!" She snapped. "I was good enough to sleep with, but that's it?"

"Are you serious, Mariah? You're sitting here crying over another man while you're supposedly carrying my child? I know things have not been perfect between us, and I expected you to do your own thing while we were apart for those few months, but what you will *not* do is sit here and disrespect me to my face!"

"Tell her, bruh," I emphasized.

"Are you even sure that's my child?" he asked, and I could hear the slight crack in his voice.

"Of course, it's yours, Gerald. How could you even ask something like that?"

"What the hell do you mean? Look at this shit you pulled!" I cut in. "You're standing up here with two men who you claimed to be pregnant by, and you gon' ask him some dumb crap like that. This man shouldn't believe a damn thing that comes out your lying ass mouth."

"Could you please shut up!"

"Don't tell him to shut up just because you don't want to hear the truth. He's right. I have every right to question whether you're being honest after all the lies you've told us both." Gerald was seething.

"This is *not* his child," she adamantly insisted. "I only told him that it was because I was upset with how he treated me and hurt my feelings. This baby is yours, Gerald. I swear."

"Oooh, bitch." I stood to my feet, shaking my head. "You should be calling my mama and thanking her for raising a decent man, because if I was anything less, I'd be beating your ass in here right about now."

I left them standing there with their mouths hanging open in shock of what I'd just said. It was the truth though. Mariah just didn't realize how bad I wanted to go upside her head.

After slamming her door shut behind me, I could hear the two of them inside arguing, but I kept it moving. That was their business, and I was just glad to have one less problem I needed to deal with.

✦

"HEYYY, HEAVEN," WAS THE FIRST THING OUT OF JORDYN'S mouth after she answered the door at Ash's crib.

"Well, hello to you too, rudeness. I guess Heaven is the only person you see standing here."

"Hey, Cello. Don't be a brat. I had to speak to juicy mama first." She laughed, letting us inside. "Where y'all been today, looking all cute in your matching jogging suits?"

"First of all, I'm a grown ass man. Ain't nothing cute about me," I joshed.

"You're right about that," she said, playfully rolling her eyes. "I was really only talking about Heaven."

"Yeah, whatever. Where your man at?"

"Down in the basement. You want me to watch her while you go down there?" she offered.

"Nah, that's okay. I brought her over to see him."

"Okay. Well, I'm about to head to the grocery store to pick up a few things to get started on dinner. Tell Ash I'll be right back," she said, grabbing her purse from the nearby table and heading to the garage.

Descending the stairs of the basement, I could hear Dave East's *P2* album playing before I made it to the bottom of the landing. I already knew that he was more than likely in the middle of one of his drawings and in his zone.

"Nigga, I know you better not be down here smoking the place out," I jokingly called out, grabbing his attention. "We not trying to smell that shit."

His face was contorted into a hard grimace as he looked up but quickly changed after seeing me carrying Heaven in my arms. His smile widened as he dropped his pencil and paused the track playing through the stereo system.

"There go Unc's big girl," he chimed as he stood to take her from me. "It's about time your ugly ass daddy brought my baby to see me."

"Don't listen to him, baby. Your ugly ass uncle knows our address." I laughed, plopping down onto the sofa across from where Ash took a seat with Heaven. "What you down here cooking up?"

"Shit. Just had a few pieces that's been floating around in my head for a minute," he said, glancing back over his shoulder toward his workstation.

"Word? You need to let me check 'em out when you're done," I told him, smiling inwardly as I watched him interacting with my baby girl. "How shit been around here? You and Jo cool?"

"Yeah, we're straight," he answered before chuckling to

himself. "That girl is something else, man, but that's my baby. I'm riding with her 'til the wheels fall off."

"You're saying that like you have a choice." I laughed. "Jo's not letting your ass go anywhere. Sis got that on lock.'

"I can't even say anything to that because you're right. I'm cool with that though. She's got me, and I got her. Jordyn's lil' ass is official. Not many chicks can keep up with my life, but she's been thuggin' it out with me and taking it all in stride."

"How's everything *else* been?" I asked.

Sighing, he positioned a sleepy Heaven on his chest before he answered. "Tough, man," he said, shaking his head. "Tough as hell. This shit been fucking with me hard, bruh."

Ash and I were extremely close, so it wasn't unusual for us to strip away our tough exteriors and be vulnerable with each other. That's why I wasn't surprised when I noticed his eyes begin to mist as he got lost in his thoughts. I didn't want to push him to talk, so I settled back into my seat as I waited for him to continue.

After sitting in silence for a few minutes, his tear-stained face turned to me, and the pain in his eyes caused me to hurt for my bro. It wasn't too often that Ash got like *this*, but when he did it was definitely something serious. Ash was quick to shut down to avoid having to face his problems. I knew he had been going through it these last few days and was still taking Brent's death hard.

Even though Brent had committed the ultimate act of betrayal toward Ash and was set on taking him out, I knew for a fact that Ash really didn't want to kill his brother. If anything, he would have done everything in his power to find another way out of the situation. I still didn't know all the details, but from the bit of information that I was able to get out of Jordyn, Ash wasn't the one that pulled the trigger on Brent. Dylan was.

"I keep replaying that night over and over again in my head, trying to figure out what I could have done differently," Ash finally said, resting his head back against the back of the couch and staring up at the ceiling.

"I should have been shut Brent down, but I didn't. I underestimated just how much he actually hated me. Out of all of the fucked-up shit I've done in my life, I don't think I could have added killing my little brother to that list, man. Don't get me wrong. I would have most definitely fucked his lil' ass up to the point where he wished he was dead. I know I said that when I caught up to him that it was a wrap, but I wasn't really going to take it there. But after shit with D," he admitted, trying to blink away his tears. "I would rather it be *me* who has to bear that shit than him. That's what's fucking with me the most, man, and I know that it's killing D. If I had just handled it, it wouldn't have gone down like that. Dylan wouldn't have been put in that position."

"You can't keep beating yourself up over that, bruh. Look, Ash, as messed up as it is, Brent knew what and who he was up against. He let jealousy and greed get in the way, and unfortunately, he had to pay for it with his life," I said, leaning forward to rest my forearms on my knees. "I can't say I know how either of you feel because I'd be lying, but wouldn't you rather you, Jo, and D still be here than us having to prepare to bury all of y'all?"

"Yeah, you're right," he said, barely audible.

We both sat in our own thoughts for a while, and I could feel him starting to retract, so I decided to redirect our conversation in an attempt to lighten the mood.

"Oh, man. I know what I meant to tell you," I spoke up, gaining his attention. "How about Mariah's ass was lying about the damn baby."

"Nigga, you lying," he said lifting his head slightly to peer over at me with wide eyes. "When you found that out?"

"The other day when I popped up on her ass at her crib."

"So she was lying about being pregnant? What the hell? Females these days be trippin'."

"Oh, she wasn't lying about that part, but the baby damn sure ain't mine," I told him and went on to explain.

"Where you be finding these broads at, man?" Ash laughed after I finished running down the story to him.

"Hell if I know. I'm about to go on strike. I'm done with this crap. These women been giving my ass the blues."

"Yeah, whatever. You talking all that shit now, but we both know yo' behind ain't giving up pussy," he said, laughing.

He was right. There was no way that was happening, but I damn sure was about to be more selective with who I messed with. Now that I had Heaven with me full-time, I had to be careful with who I let into my space.

"What Faye say when she found out?" Ash asked, breaking me from my thoughts.

"Nothing. I haven't told her a damn thing." I shrugged.

"Why not? I figured that would have been the first person you told."

"For what?" My face frowned up. "Faye and I weren't even together, and she still flipped on me like I righteously did something wrong. If she would have stuck around to see how shit played out, she would've known she didn't even have a reason to be."

"I feel you on that, but damn. I thought y'all was finally starting to get somewhere. Y'all asses were going on dates and shit."

I chuckled. "Man, we were just chilling as friends. That's it. Shit was cool, but I'm not about to chase behind Fatima. If we're meant to be in each other's lives, then we will be. If not, I'll just have to live with that."

"I know that's—What's up, Jo? You need something?" he

asked, stopping mid-sentence and turning to face where she stood by the entrance.

I glanced her way too. I didn't hear her come down and wasn't sure how long she'd been standing there, but it was no surprise to me that Ash had picked up on her presence before she even got the chance to make it known.

"Oh... umm... sorry. Didn't mean to interrupt, babe. Just wanted to let you know that the food will be done in a minute," she told Ash and turned to me. "You and baby girl staying for dinner?"

"Hell yeah. What type of question is that?" I joked. "Only home-cooked meals a nigga gets is when I'm crashing Ma Dukes' crib or Shan's. I already know you up there throwing down."

"Well, you could be eating like this every day," she commented with a nonchalant shrug of her shoulders, but I caught the subliminal shots she was sending.

"Yeah, you're right. I guess we just need to start coming over here every day for dinner. What time we need to be here?" I asked.

"Don't play, Cello. You know what I meant," she said, frowning slightly. "Why—"

"We'll be up in a second, baby. Thank you," Ash said, coming to my rescue before she could start with her onslaught of questions.

Jordyn's stubborn behind wanted to say more, but I guess Ash's subtle dismissal got the job done. Rolling her eyes in my direction, she turned on her heels and retreated up the stairs.

"Who is that? Because it damn sure wasn't the Jordyn I know," I asked jokingly. "Did she really just walk away without putting up a fight?"

"You better get off my baby, man. We're making progress around here," he said, laughing along with me. "You should be thanking me because you know she was two seconds from going in on your butt. You know her lil' sneaky behind heard that mess you said about old girl and the whole baby situation. Bet money she ran her tail straight upstairs to run her mouth to Faye."

"Whatever. That's their business. Like I said, I'm not about to chase her. If Fatima wants to talk, she knows where to find me."

9

ASH

"Ashley, are you listening to anything I'm saying?"

Sighing, I massaged my stiff neck before bringing my eyes up to meet my uncle's. I had zero interest in what he was talking about, but I nodded my head. For the past hour or so, Unc had been talking my head off, and to be honest, I hadn't been paying attention to a damn thing he said since he started.

"No the hell you aren't," Unc barked, causing me to groan. "I don't care about all that huffing and puffing, son, so you can keep it. This shit with you and your pops needs to be squashed. We lay your brother to rest tomorrow, and I don't want any shit from you two."

"I could care less about that motherfucker. I'm chilling. You should be having this conversation with his ass since he's the one talking slick and sending shots," I told him.

"You have to understand that he just lost a son, Ash. He's lashing out," Unc said, coming to his defense.

"So the fuck what! I lost a brother! The same brother who's been trying to put a bullet in my head," I yelled, growing upset. "Where the fuck was our *pops* at then? Why wasn't he telling his damn son to chill the fuck out? I'll tell you why. It's because he was hoping that nigga succeeded. He's only using this as an excuse, because just like Brent, Pops doesn't have a reason why he hates me so damn much either. I'm done letting shit ride, Unc. If he wants war with me, I'ma bring that shit to him. He's coming at me like I'm the one that killed B. If he—"

"What?" Unc asked, cutting me off. "What the hell are you talking about, Ash? Didn't you?"

I cursed to myself and ran my hands down my face. The only people outside of the ones who were present that knew what went down in the warehouse that night were Morgan and Marcel... and Fatima. As far as I was concerned, it was no one's business who actually pulled the trigger.

Everyone was already set on believing that I was the one behind Brent's death, and I didn't care enough to tell them otherwise. Besides, I would rather it be me to have to deal with whatever consequences that may arise behind the incident than for Dylan to.

"Answer me, Ashley!"

"What does it matter?" I yelled back. "Either way people are going to believe what they want. Just let it go, Unc."

"I will not let it go! I want answers!" he retorted. "Wait. D and the girl were there, too. Did she do this? Is that why you won't say anything? Are you protecting her, Ashley? If she had anything to do with this, I swear—"

"Unc, I swear on mine and your life if the next words out of your mouth were about to be a threat to my woman, I won't hesitate to drop you," I growled coldly. "Jordyn didn't do shit. If she did, she would have been well within her right. The mother-fucker kidnapped her and would have killed her."

"Well, what else am I supposed to believe if you refuse to tell me anything? If you're claiming you didn't, and she's not—"

He stopped talking, and I knew the exact moment it all started to make sense to him.

Staring off into space, he blindly reached behind him for a chair before plopping down into it. He sat shaking his head in disbelief for a while before looking up to meet my eyes.

"Man, not Dylan, Ashley," he said in disbelief. "Dylan didn't, did he?"

I didn't bother to answer what he already knew. Instead, I simply shrugged. "He wasn't left with much choice, now was he? He did what he had to do."

"But he shouldn't have had—"

"But he did. Look, Unc. I'm done talking about this. What's done is done. I'm tired and would rather be getting myself mentally prepared to deal with tomorrow. If we're done here, I'm about to dip," I told him, already preparing to head for the door.

"Ash." He stopped me before I could leave. "Just think about what I said, son. At the end of the day, he's still your father."

⚜

MY HEAD ROSE AT THE SOUND OF THE BEDROOM DOOR BEING pushed open. The light from the hall cast a slight glow into the dark room and illuminated Jordyn's silhouette in the doorway.

She smiled meekly in my direction as she pulled the door back closed behind her and quietly entered further into the room.

"Hey," she spoke lowly, glancing in my direction briefly before heading straight for the bathroom.

"*Hey?*" I scoffed behind her, standing from my position at the edge of the bed. "What was that? You mad at me or something?"

"No, of course not. Why would you think that?" she asked in confusion.

"Umm, that dry ass 'hey' is why I would think that. What's wrong?" I asked, approaching her and pulling her to me.

"Nothing, Ashley. I just figured you were having one of your moments and needed some space. I wasn't trying to intrude on your alone time. I just needed to shower and get my things ready for tomorrow."

At the mention of the next day, she dropped her gaze and nervously began to fidget with her hands.

"Hey," I said, lifting her chin to look into her eyes. "Baby, you know you don't have to come with me, right? I know it'll probably be too much—"

"Yes, I do," she stated adamantly. "You need me there, so that's where I'm going to be. No, I'm not too thrilled about going, but I'll just have to suck it up."

I nodded and decided to drop it. There was no point in trying to change her mind. I knew that Jordyn really wasn't feeling going to the funeral, but she was dead set on being there to support me. Truth be told, I really didn't want to go either, but I couldn't *not* show my face.

"Are you ready?" Jordyn asked, breaking into my thoughts.

Sighing, I ran my hands through my hair and gave her question some thought. "Honestly, baby, I don't think this is some shit I could ever be ready for. Regardless of the situation, burying *any* of my brothers just isn't something I want to have to do."

"I know it may not really mean much, but I'm with you every step of the way," she told me.

"Nah, ma," I said, leaning down to place a gentle kiss on her lips. "That shit means everything."

THE SECOND I STEPPED FOOT THROUGH THE CHURCH DOORS, eyes were on me as I made my way to the front of the church with Jordyn right beside me and Marcel following not too far behind.

I was sure everyone probably thought I wouldn't show since I chose not to ride with the family, especially Morgan. I saw the surprised look on his face the moment he noticed us entering the church. Morgan stood as we approached the front row and pulled me into a tight hug.

"I thought you changed your mind," he said lowly so only I could hear.

"I gave you my word, didn't I?" I grumbled as we pulled away, and I turned to Dylan, who stood next to him.

I pulled him to me by the back of his head and threw my arms around him. The sadness in his eyes told me that he was having a hard time facing the day as well. Deciding not to hold up service any longer than we already had, we all took our seats and gave the pastor our attention.

Feeling someone staring at me, I turned until I locked eyes with none other than my pops. From the look on his face, it was obvious that he wasn't too excited about my presence. Too bad for him I didn't give a damn.

I guessed Jordyn noticed the staring match that we were having and squeezed my hand to gain my attention. It took everything in me to tear my eyes away, but I finally turned and faced her. Her concerned expression met mine as her eyebrows raised, inquiring if I was okay. I nodded and brought her hand up to kiss the back of it before facing forward.

By the time I realized what was going on, the pastor was giving his closing remarks. I had been on autopilot during the entire service and had completely zoned out. I was just ready for it all to be over with. I was simply going through the motions of it all. By the time I decided to check back in and join everyone else, we were already at the cemetery where everyone had gathered to say their final goodbyes.

"This shit still doesn't feel real," Dylan commented as we stood off to the side sharing a blunt.

"I know." I sighed and turned to face him. "How you doing though, bruh? I mean like *really*."

Massaging the back of his neck, he cast his gaze down toward the ground and shrugged. "I don't even know, Ash. I'm not sure how I'm supposed to feel. Is it fucked up that out of everything, the biggest thing I'm feeling is relief? I don't even have to ask that, because I know it is, but right is right. I loved B, man, but I couldn't sit by and let that shit happen. I did what I had to do, and I can live with that. It just fucks with me that I didn't catch this shit. Me and bruh fucking lived together and were together damn near all the time."

"Aye, let that go, D. You and B had your own lives to live. You couldn't keep up with his every move. Let's just move forward," I told him, glancing over at Jordyn for the hundredth time as she stood talking to Marcel.

"You're right." He nodded and then stopped to follow my gaze. "You feeling lil' baby, huh?"

"Something like that," I answered, trying to conceal the smile that threatened my features.

"Yeah, whatever. Look at you," he said, nudging me. "Over there cheesing and shit. She got your nose wide open. You ain't took your eyes off her this whole time. It's okay, bruh. She not about to disappear."

"Man, shut yo' ass up, and gone somewhere." I laughed and playfully pushed him away from me as Morgan came over to join us.

"What y'all boys over here talking about?" he questioned as he took the outstretched blunt from Dylan.

"This in love ass nigga." Dylan chuckled as he nodded in my direction.

"Bruh, chill. Ain't nobody say shit about love," I told him.

"Ain't have to say it." Morgan laughed too. "Yo' actions speaking for you, and them hoes yelling loud as hell that you love that damn girl."

"Man, whatever." I waved them off. "I'm about to dip, though. In the meantime, y'all boys need to find y'all some business."

I ignored them while they continued to clown me as I walked away in Jordyn's direction. "You ready to roll, baby?" I asked, kissing the top of her head.

"Whenever you are."

"Cool," I said and turned to Marcel to dap him up. "'Preciate you being here today, bruh."

"You already know I got you, man," he said. "What y'all about to get into?"

"Shit. About to grab something to eat before dropping Jo off at Faye's. I got some shit I need to handle."

"Word? Everything good? You need me to roll with you?" he asked with a raised brow.

"Nah, man. Nothing like that," I assured him. "Just something I need to do."

"Aight. Well, I'll get at y'all later," he said, hugging Jordyn. "I'm about to go scoop my lil' mama from Ma Dukes'. I know she's driving her crazy by now."

Jordyn and I were headed toward the car, but I felt her stop before pulling her hand from my grasp and rushing over to where Dylan was still standing. Jordyn hadn't really been around my brothers but a handful of times, so I was a little confused as to what she was doing.

Watching on, it surprised me when she went in to hug him, drawing him into a tight embrace. His eyes widened at first, and he looked over her head toward me, but I only shrugged in return as I walked closer to them. After a few seconds of standing there awkwardly, he finally decided to hug her back.

I didn't feel any type of way as I stood to the side and watched the exchange. Something was telling me that they both needed that. Jordyn pulled back and wiped her face.

"Thank you, Dylan," she told him, attempting to blink away tears that threatened to fall. "I never got to tell you that. Really... thank you, and I'm sorry about what I said to you that day in the car. You're a great brother to Ash. I probably wouldn't be standing here right now if you weren't."

"It's nothing, ma. We're good. You were just looking out for my brother, and I appreciate that. I'm glad he has someone like you," Dylan told her. "You're a real one, shorty."

"That she is," Morgan agreed. "Don't hesitate to hit my line if this knucklehead gets out of line. If you need *anything*, we got you, ma. You're family now."

⊗⊗⊗

It had been a couple hours since I dropped Jordyn off, and I was still aimlessly roaming the streets, contemplating if I wanted to make my next move. I drove in silence as I headed to my destination.

There wasn't much room for me to change my mind because it took me no time to get to where I was going. I didn't care that my visit was unannounced and surely unwanted.

"Sir, you can't just walk in there! I'll ask if—"

"Bruh, back yo' ass up, and get out my way. I don't need permission to do shit," I barked at my father's assistant before bursting through his office doors. "My nigga, we need to talk, so send yo' lil' flunkies on somewhere."

He nodded his head toward his assistant and dismissed him

from the room. "Well, that was quite the entrance. You'll have to excuse my son, gentlemen," he said to the men sitting across from his desk. He was obviously amused by my abrupt intrusion. "We can talk later, Ashley. I'm in the middle of business as you can see."

"No, we can talk right now," I replied calmly, removing my gun from my waist. "I don't give a damn what you're in the middle of. I'm not asking."

Releasing a pissed off chuckle, my pops eyed me before turning to his companions.

"Gentlemen, we can resume this meeting another time," he said to his guests. "It's obvious my son needs some attention at the moment. Stop by and schedule another appointment with Joseph on your way out. Whatever time is best for you."

I watched as the men quickly gathered their belongings without so much as a glance in my direction. With how quickly they exited the office, it was evident they didn't want any of the problems I was bringing.

Once we were alone, I approached my pops' desk and stared him down. "I let those weak ass subliminal shots you've been sending my way ride. I even promised your brother I'd let you live after knowing for a fact you were the one behind our spot getting burned down. I don't know what type of bullshit you on, but you need to stand the fuck down before shit gets ugly. You *really* don't want to take it there with me."

"Son, we can take it where ever you want to take it," he replied coolly, leaning back in his seat. "I'm starting to believe you've forgotten who the hell I am and what I'm capable of. Your threats hold no weight here."

"And I'm starting to realize that you never really knew who *I* am or what I'm *truly* capable of," I barked back, leaning down on his desk. "This ain't back in your day. A lot of shit has changed around here, including who's running these streets. I don't have time to have a pissing contest with you, but if you even *think* you can come at me, you might want to check my resume first. This is my first and only warning. Find something safe to do, and stay the fuck out the way. If I have to come see you again, my bullets gon' greet you first."

Not bothering to stick around to hear any more of the bull-shit that was sure to come out his mouth, I turned and prepared to make my exit. I'd said all that I had to say. It was on him whether he chose to listen and take my warning seriously, which was very unlikely, but I was prepared for that.

"It was nice talking to you, son." He chuckled from behind me before I could make it out the door. "We'll be seeing each other again very soon. I'll be sure to bring *my* resume with me."

10

JORDYN

Stretching my limbs across the bed, I blindly searched the space beside me for Ash. My eyes popped open after coming up empty, but I relaxed after remembering where I was. After leaving Grams' earlier, Fatima and I had come back to her spot, and my behind had hopped straight in the bed.

Glancing over at the clock on the nightstand, I realized that I had slept the entire evening away, and it was damn near eight o'clock at night. I hadn't realized I was so exhausted. Pulling my phone from the charger, I checked it to see the missed calls and texts that I had from none other than Ash.

"Hey, baby." I yawned into the receiver after returning his call.

"What's up, sleepyhead? I see you finally decided to wake your butt up."

"I was so tired. I didn't even realize I was out like that. I'm surprised Faye didn't come wake me up."

"Oh, she tried. I sent her in there to make sure you were good after you didn't answer. You were knocked out, ma," he said, laughing. "You needed that rest, though. Now that you're out of your coma, what y'all about to get into?"

"I'm not sure. It's getting late now. I probably messed up whatever plans we might've had. We might still grab something to eat."

"Cool. Let me know if y'all do end up getting out, and hit me if you need anything," he said before we ended our call.

Climbing out of bed, I headed straight for the bathroom to release my bladder before going to find Fatima. She was sitting on the couch staring down at something on her laptop while stuffing her face with Gelato.

"Hey, honey." I yawned.

"It's about time you got up. You in there sleeping like you're pregnant or something," she joshed.

"Girl, whatever. I was tired," I told her, taking a seat. "What you over there doing?"

"Looking at a few buildings and waiting on you to wake up," she said, sitting her laptop beside her.

"Buildings? For what?"

"Just trying to get a feel for what prices would look like. Hey, what do you think about me opening my own salon?"

"Oh my God, Faye! That would be dope as hell," I exclaimed excitedly. "I *know* you can make it happen, but what made you want to do that? Where'd this come from?"

"I don't know," she shrugged. "I've been thinking about it for a minute now and figured why not. I mean, I practically run things down at Janet's place. I could be putting that energy into building my own. Plus, it'll be something that I actually put in the hard work to make happen, something I can be proud of. After the whole Kyle situation, I really had to sit down and do some serious thinking. Other than Mama's medical bills, I was throwing all that money away. You just don't know how much money I've had in my hands."

"Oh, baby, with all the Gucci and other name brand shit in your closet, I think I do." I laughed.

"And that's just it. All that material shit is all I have to show for it. Now, I'm stuck with nothing trying to figure out what I'm going to do with this high ass apartment once my lease is up. I damn sure can't afford it. Luckily, the car is paid for, but the insurance is still kicking my ass."

"What the hell, Faye? You weren't at least putting any money to the side in your savings? You had to have known that thing with you and Kyle wasn't going to last forever."

"I knew that, Jo. I just thought I'd have enough time to get it together. I wasn't expecting things with Marcel to happen. That threw everything off," she replied, shaking her head sadly. "Now, look at me. Everything's all messed up." She sniffled.

"You okay, Faye?" I asked, snuggling next to her.

"Yes, Jordyn." She sighed, trying her best not to shed anymore tears. "I'm good. I knew better and should have just let both of those situations go, especially Marcel. I don't even know why I thought we could be friends after all that went down. I was too busy trying to hold on to something that wasn't there anymore."

"Come on, Faye. Don't do that. What you and Cello have is—"

"*Had*, Jo," she corrected me. "As much as I wanted to believe that we were working toward getting back together, I knew that probably wasn't going to happen. I know Marcel, and he's the type to hold grudges. I can't see him ever getting over everything that happened with Kyle. He probably did all of this to get back at me and wanted to hurt me like I hurt him."

"Okay, Fatima. You're tripping now. You know that doesn't even sound like Cello."

"All I know is that there's a woman walking around claiming to be pregnant by him, and it's not me," she told me, wiping away a few tears that managed to escape. "I just can't deal with that, Jo. If anybody should be carrying his child, it should be me."

I wrapped my arms around her and allowed her to rest her head on my shoulder. "Have you at least talked to him? You didn't stick around to know if this chick was even telling the truth."

"It doesn't matter. It still doesn't change the fact that instead of trying to work things out between us, he was too busy hopping in the next bitch's bed. I'm good on Marcel."

"But, Faye, she's not—"

"Leave it alone, Jordyn. I'm tired of talking about it because it's not going to do anything but get me upset, and I'm tired of crying over him."

Even though Fatima and Marcel were indeed broken up at the time that he had supposedly gotten this woman pregnant, it still didn't soften the blow to her heart. I swear I wanted to kill his ass for breaking my aunt's heart, but I couldn't really be too mad at him. I might have been on Fatima's side and was going to ride for her until the wheels fell off, but she brought this on herself.

As if right on cue, Fatima's phone rang, causing her to groan in response. I already had a good idea of who it was since they had been blowing her phone up last night too. Instead of continuing to ignore them, she decided to go ahead and answer.

"Yes, Kyle." She sighed out of irritation, placing the call on speaker.

"Ah. It's about time you answered. Are you ready to talk to me now?"

"About what, Kyle? I already said what I had to say. I'm trying to figure out why you insist on continuing to call me after I made it clear that I was done with our little *arrangement*," she retorted, rolling her eyes to the ceiling.

The creepy ass chuckle that came flowing through the phone made my skin crawl.

"Fatima, sweetheart, our *arrangement*, as you put it, isn't done until *I* say it is. I'm not finished with you yet," he stated. "I was patient enough and gave you your space to get whatever that little phase you called yourself going through with that hoodlum out of your system. I'm willing to forgive you and look past that."

"Excuse me? *Forgive me?*" She reared back and stared at the phone. "Okay, Kyle. I don't know what kind of drugs you've been experimenting with, but you're out of your damn mind. Stop calling my phone."

She disconnected the call and tossed the phone on the table in front of us. The audacity of that fool. I had never met Kyle a day in my life and only knew of him what little Fatima told me. However, none of that mattered. If he kept talking to my aunt like he was crazy, his ass was going to get dealt with.

"Why is it so hard for his ass to take a hint?" I asked.

"Hell if I know. I'm going to have to get a restraining order against his behind or something." She huffed.

"Or I could just get Ash to handle him for you. I'm sure he'd stop bothering you then."

"Yeah, I'm pretty damn sure he would too, Jordyn. I want the man to go away, but I'm not trying to get him killed," she told me. "Thanks, but no thanks. I can handle Kyle on my own."

"Hey, if you say so, but the offer's there in case you change your mind." I shrugged.

"I'll keep that in mind, Jo," she said, shaking her head at me. "You staying over again tonight?"

"I hadn't planned on it. I was going back to Ash's, but I can if you want me to."

She waved me off and shook her head. "No, you're good. I

was just asking. Go ahead to your man. You already know his spoiled ass would have been showing up in the middle of the night to come get you anyway. He was cool for one night, but two might be pushing it."

I laughed along with her because I knew she was telling the truth.

"Ash will be okay," I assured her. "How about we go out tonight or something? It's been like forever and we both could use a few drinks."

"I don't know, Jo. I'm not really in the mood to be around a crowd right now. Hell, we can grab a bottle and drink here."

"Nooo, Faye." I whined. "I want to get out. I've been stressed as hell. We both have. Come on. We don't have to stay out long."

"Jordyn, I don't have anything to wear," she said, trying to come up with whatever excuse she could to get out of going out tonight.

Her response only caused me to side-eye her and fold my arms across my chest. "With as much as your little sugar daddy was caking you and taking you shopping, I know that's a damn lie. So get your behind up, and let's find something to wear."

"Ugh," she groaned, standing to her feet and heading toward her bedroom. "You know you're just as bossy as your ugly ass boyfriend."

"Girl, boo. My baby might be a lot of things, but ugly damn sure ain't never been one of them," I retorted. "Now, move your booty, and let's find you a bad ass fit so we can go shut the city down."

❦

"DANG, LOOK AT THAT LINE, JO. AIN'T NO WAY WE'RE ABOUT

to get in," Fatima groaned. "It's wrapped around the damn building."

"And? We're not about to wait in it. Come on," I said, grabbing her hand and pulling her behind me.

I noticed the ugly looks that a few people waiting in line sent our way as I led us straight up to the bouncer.

"What's up, Mac?" I chimed, giving him a quick hug.

"What's good, lil' Jordyn? What you doing down here? My man know you out here like this?" he asked, eyeing both of our attire.

Folding my arms across my chest with attitude and cocking my head to the side, I glanced down at our outfits as well. "Out here like what?" I asked but didn't let him answer. "Ash is my man, not my daddy. You got us or what?"

"Yeah, man," he said, shaking his head and stepping to the side. "Aye, they're good."

The other bouncer that was standing with him nodded his head and continued to search everyone before allowing them to make their way inside.

"Good looking out, Mac," I told him.

"You know I got you, but don't be in there showing your ass," he advised.

As soon as we stepped inside, the bass from the speakers consumed my body and caused my chest to rattle. It was all the way live in here. It was so packed inside that I wasn't sure where the hell all those people in line thought they were going.

"See. Nuh uh, we could have just gone to a bar or something. It's too damn packed in here. A bitch can barely move," Fatima complained, trying to push her way through the crowd and keep up with me as I headed straight for the bar.

"Faye, I'm not about to sit here and listen to you complain all night," I told her, flagging down the bartender. "We need to hurry up and get some drinks in you."

Rolling her eyes in my direction, she turned to scope out the crowd while I ordered some shots. As soon as they were in my possession, I was damn near forcing the strong liquor down her throat, followed by another. I had to loosen her ass up.

"You see anywhere to sit? I damn sure don't, and in a minute, I doubt if I'm still going to be able to stand!" Fatima yelled over the music at me as I passed her a mixed drink.

We were both still searching the thick crowd with our eyes, but it seemed we were both coming up short. I felt my face frown up as a figure stood in front of us blocking our lines of vision.

"You looking for me, gorgeous?" a deep voice asked, causing my eyes to trail up his torso until they landed on his face.

His eyes were zoomed in on Fatima, but her eyes were squinted at him while her face held the same expression mine had a few seconds ago. Even though my initial thought was to go off on him, I couldn't deny that the brother was definitely easy on the eyes. Plus, he seemed to be checking for Fatima, so I was going to fall back and see how things played out.

"Nah, I wasn't. Can you move? You're blocking my view," Fatima said, dismissing him.

"Well, damn. Who pissed in your Cheerios? Smile, baby girl." Old boy chuckled, standing in the same spot.

"Maybe I don't feel like smiling, and maybe I don't feel like having a nigga all up in my face," she growled at him.

My mouth slightly dropped open at her bluntness. I couldn't believe she was handling this man like this.

"You too pretty to be acting all mean. Whoever the nigga was that dirted you sure did mess you up for the next man. That bitter shit unattractive as fuck," he said, shaking his head as he walked away and left her standing there with her mouth hanging wide open.

As soon as he walked away, I grabbed her hand and whipped

her around in my direction. She was steady fussing about me almost making her fall, but I didn't care about any of that.

"Girl, what the hell is wrong with you?" I queried. "You did not have to snap at that man like that. He was only trying to get your crabby ass to stop standing there looking like you smelled shit."

"Forget him," she said, frowning. "I'm not trying to be dealing with any more men. Hell, I think I might just want to go gay."

"I know you're still pissed about Marcel and all, but now, you sound dumb. You can't just *go* gay. I'm not sure it works like that."

"Whatever. If all these other confused hoes can do it, so can I. It's settled. I'm gay now. From now on, I only fuck with bad bitches."

"Oh, that's how we doing it?" some chick passing us stopped to ask, eyeing Fatima seductively.

"Baby, don't pay her any attention. She's drunk," I told her, shooing the chick along. "I'm not about to fool with you, Faye. That damn girl was ready to snatch you up quick."

"Hell, she could have. She was thick as hell too. Don't be trying to block," Fatima said.

"Shut up, crazy. Here." I laughed and shoved a new drink in her hand.

"You talking about I'm drunk, but you still feeding me drinks," she said, but still downed her drink. "Come on. I see a free table over this way."

Before we could head in the direction where she'd just pointed, our path was blocked yet again. My eyes trailed up their body until I was face to face with features eerily similar to Ash's, causing my face to frown instantly. It still creeped me out exactly how much the men in Ash's family resembled each other.

"May I help you?" I asked. I was irritated and honestly a little rattled.

"I'm sure you can, gorgeous," Ash's father responded, licking his lips at me. "I don't think we've had the pleasure of being formally introduced."

"And I don't think an introduction is needed. Are you going to get to the point of you being in my face, or are you going to continue wasting my time?" I rudely asked.

Forget the pleasantries. I didn't have anything to say to this man. If my man didn't fool with him, then neither did I.

"Yep. You're definitely Ashley's girl." He laughed. "You and my son both have that flip ass mouth in common."

From the stories that Ash had told me about him, I was tempted to go upside his head, and I would have if he hadn't looked like the woman-beater type.

"His *woman*," I corrected him. "Look, you and I have nothing to discuss, so I'm not sure why you're even over here."

He chuckled as he openly eye-fucked me. "Oh, we have a lot to discuss. My son seems to not know his place. He's also taken something away from me that I unfortunately can never get back," he said, his eyes turning dark.

"Sorry, but that has nothing to do with me."

He laughed menacingly. "Sweetheart, in this life, you'll learn that it has *everything* to do with you," he said coldly. "You might want to let Ashley know that he's not as invincible as he thinks he is. You better enjoy each other while you can. I expect to be seeing him soon."

"How about you let him know yourself? I'm sure just like you found me, you can find him. Matter of fact, I'll give you his number if you don't have it, and you can call him," I said, grabbing Fatima's hand and pulling her closer to my side. "Sorry, but I don't have any more time to waste on talking to you. You enjoy the rest of your night."

11

ASH

"Ashley!"

My head snapped up at the sound of Jordyn's voice, and I could hear from the urgency in her tone that something was wrong.

"I'm in my office," I called out, getting up to meet her. As soon as I swung my door open, she fell right into my arms. "Aye, what's wrong, Jo?"

"Your dad approached me tonight while Faye and I were out, and—"

"Wait. What?" I said, pushing her away from me so that I could examine her. "You good? What did he say to you? Did he touch you?"

"I'm fine, Ash. He just spooked me," she said. "He said some crazy junk about enjoying each other while we can and that he'd be expecting to see you soon. Ash, I'm not green to this shit. I *know* he was sending you a message and not a nice one. I could tell by the way he was looking at me."

She was absolutely right. I knew my pops, and I knew how

he operated. Him going to Jordyn instead of me was a clear message. It was a fuckboy move, but it was a message nonetheless. Father or not, I wouldn't hesitate to dead that nigga if he so much as breathed wrong in Jordyn's direction.

Pulling Jordyn into my chest, I kissed the top of her head and held her. "Don't worry about that, ma. I'll handle it," I assured her.

"But—"

"I said I'll handle it, baby. Leave it at that," I told her.

If it wasn't one thing, it was another. I was starting to think bullshit was just becoming a permanent fixture in my life. I couldn't seem to shake it.

"Listen, go upstairs, and I'll come run you a bath. Okay?"

"Can you get in with me?" She gazed up at me with sad eyes.

"You can get that, ma. Come on," I said, tapping her backside and nudging her toward the direction of the stairs.

As I sat in the massive tub with Jordyn cradled in my lap, I allowed my mind to wonder. It still tripped me out that the woman sitting on me had grown to mean so much to me over such a short period of time.

Staring down into her chocolate face, I admired her beauty. Jordyn had completely shaken up my world. Everything I thought I knew and thought I wanted was no more. I didn't want to go as far as saying she changed me, but she definitely gave me a new outlook on life and what I wanted out of it.

I laughed to myself, thinking of how glad I was that I decided not to kill her little mean ass that first night we met. Now, she had me sitting here prepared to off any and everybody that even thought to bring harm her way, including my own blood.

"What are you thinking about?" she questioned, shifting in my lap until she was straddling me.

"You," I replied, looking at her through hooded eyes.

She blushed under my penetrating gaze and avoided looking at me. She loved acting like she was shy when we both knew that was a damn lie.

"Jo," I called, turning her chin back in my direction. "You know I love you, right? Like *really* love you."

I watched her eyes buck as she struggled to find the right words. I knew my declaration took her by surprise, and honestly, I shocked myself. My feelings for Jordyn always scared me because of how intense they were. Even when I tried to pull away, I still couldn't run from them. Whether Jordyn knew it or not, she had me. All of me.

"Jordyn?"

"I love you too, Ash," she said, grabbing my face and pressing her lips firmly against mine before slipping her tongue between my lips.

"Mmm," she moaned, grinding her hips in my lap subtly.

Draining the water from the tub, I stepped out with Jordyn still in my arms and wrapped a huge towel around us as I carried her to my bed. Tossing her onto the center of it, I smirked at the seductive smile plastered on her face. Jordyn's little ass loved that rough shit.

Grabbing a hold to one of her ankles, I pulled her down to the edge of the bed toward me and flipped her onto her stomach. She glanced over her shoulder at me, anticipating what was to come. She already knew what was about to go down. I just hoped baby was ready for the ride.

৩৯৩

LEANING AGAINST THE HOOD OF MY CAR, I LOOKED OUT OVER the lake as I exhaled a thick cloud of smoke into the air.

Reflecting back on the past couple of months, I shook my head thinking about all the events that had taken place. I swear, I was ready to put all this behind me. .

Out of all my years of being in the streets, I had never been faced with some shit like that. Yeah, there was always someone that was going to be lurking in the shadows ready to take me out, but never before had those same motherfuckers been my own kin.

My attention went to the set of headlights that approached me and came to a stop. They cut the engine and stepped out, coming to a halt in front of me.

"What's up, bro?" Dylan asked as he stood before me with his arms folded across his chest. "What you call me out here for, bruh?"

"Where's Morg?"

"I don't know. I haven't been able to reach him. What's this about?"

"I just wanted to let you know that you're about to be burying your pops next," I said seriously, looking him dead in his eyes.

"What? What are you talking about, Ash?"

"I'm talking about the fact that this motherfucker won't let this shit go, and now, he's threatened Jordyn," I advised him. "I'm telling you right now, Dylan. I'm not holding back anymore."

Sighing, he ran his hands over his head and looked to the sky. "Man, Ash. When does this shit stop? We just had to bury our fucking brother, man."

"Don't you think I know that?" I barked. "I didn't ask for this shit, Dylan, but I'm gon' end it."

"Ash, bro, there's other ways to handle this. Let this one go, man. Please."

"I can't, D. He came at Jo. I'm not letting this ride. He obviously didn't take my warning serious. You can figure those *other ways* out, and let me know what you come up with," I stated sarcastically. "I just thought I should give you the courtesy of a heads up."

Tossing the butt of my blunt to the ground, I rounded the front of my whip and hopped inside. Before I could place my car in drive, tapping at my window caused me to groan before I rolled it down.

"Don't do anything crazy, Ash. Whether you fuck with that nigga or not, that's still our pops, bro," Dylan said, trying to reason with me.

"And I'm willing to bet my life that that little fact doesn't mean a damn thing to him. I'll get at you later, D. Go home."

Without another word, my foot pressed down on the accelerator, and I was out, leaving Dylan standing there staring at my lights.

Glancing down at my ringing phone, I chose not to answer after seeing that it was Jordyn calling for the hundredth time. I knew she would to be hitting my line after waking up and realizing that I wasn't there. Even though I was 100 percent sure that she was going to spaz on me for ignoring her, I would have to deal with her later. I was in my zone, and there was business to tend to.

Boom!

Bursting into my pops' man cave, I allowed my twin Desert Eagles to lead the way into the room. I was pretty certain that he was anticipating my visit after the little stunt he pulled. My pops wasn't a rookie when it came to this shit, so I was positive that he knew the exact moment I stepped into his spot.

Instead of taking my last warning serious, he chose to let

arrogance get in the way of logic. We both knew that it wasn't a social call, but he still seemed unfazed at the sight of me and actually smirked at a nigga.

"I heard you sent for me, pussy, so here I am," I announced, raising my piece and letting off two shots in his direction, hitting him once in the shoulder and again in the chest.

The impact of my hollow tips caused his body to rock backward in his seat, and he had no time to prepare for my assault. I could have easily put a bullet in his head and went on about my day.

"What the fuck, Ashley!"

My focus had been so keen on my Pops that I hadn't even paid attention to the fact that Morgan was sitting right there across from him. No wonder Dylan and I couldn't get in touch with his ass.

He hopped up from his seat and was about to approach me, but my gun pointed at his head halted all movement.

"My nigga, have you lost your fucking mind?" Morgan's anger-filled eyes glared at me in confusion. "Ash, you better get that shit out my face!"

I didn't even bother to look at Morgan. Instead, I kept my eyes trained on our punk ass daddy.

"I told you my bullets would be doing the talking if I had to come see you again. You thought I was bullshittin'?" I asked, grilling my pops.

"So you're going to kill me, Ashley? You think you're bad, huh?" he taunted as blood spurted from his mouth, and he struggled to breathe.

"Ashley!" Morgan said from beside me. "Put that shit down! You just shot our —"

"Shut the fuck up, Morgan! I don't want to hear that shit," I barked. "Fuck him! I'm done playing these fucking games with you motherfuckers. This is the Ashley y'all wanted, so this is what y'all get. Say whatever it is you have to say to this pussy now. It's a wrap for your pops."

"I'm not about to let you kill *our* damn father, Ashley! I'm going to tell you one more time—"

"You not about to *let* me?" I questioned, laughing cynically. "My nigga, it's already done."

Blood spattered the walls before either of them could process what was happening. Morgan looked on in disbelief as he stared at the large hole that marred our father's face.

The entire time, my other gun stayed trained on Morgan, causing him to look from it to me. I could see the pain in his eyes from having to witness me take our father out. There was rage there also, but instead of acting on it, he stared me in the eyes.

"So what's next, Ashley? You going to kill me too?" he asked with pain evident in his voice.

My chest tightened at the thought. "If I have to," I answered truthfully.

"When does this stop, Ashley?"

"I don't know, but I'm tired of this shit, Morgan. I'm not about to be looking over my shoulder every two seconds wondering which one of my fucking family is going to try to take me out next, and I'm damn sure not about to let another motherfucker hurt Jordyn. I love you to death, Morg, and would lay down my life for you," I told him, allowing my tears to fall freely. "But this has to end. If I can't trust you, just let me know, and we can handle this now."

"Are you seriously asking me that shit?" he asked with his nostrils flaring. "When have I even given you a reason to question my loyalty to you? Never! I'm your brother!"

"And so was Brent! And that motherfucker leaking over there was my father, so what's your point?"

"Ashley—"

"Can I trust you, Morgan!" I yelled emotionally.

"With your life, Ashley," he said, allowing a few tears of his own to escape.

Morgan and I were extremely close, and I honestly never really felt that I needed to question his loyalty. However, with everything going on, he had to understand my hesitancy. I didn't know who to believe anymore or what to think.

Lowering my gun, I cast one last look in my father's direction before turning to exit. I didn't speak another word to Morgan as I made my way to the door.

"Ash," Morgan called from behind me, but I didn't stop. "Ashley!"

⚜

"Jo," I said softly into Jordyn's ear. "Jo, wake up, baby girl."

"Hmmm," she groaned in her sleep as she swatted me away.

Reaching under the covers, my hand began to roam over her legs until I finally brought it up to settle between her thick thighs and caressed her sensitive nub.

"Wake up, shorty, or I'm going to leave you here," I told her nibbling on her neck.

"Leave me here?" she grumbled, coming to slowly. "Where are you going? Better yet, where have you been?"

She was fully awake and turned over in my arms until we were facing each other.

"Out handling business."

"You're always *handling business*," she retorted.

"That's what busy people do. Handle business. Now, you plan on getting up, or what? We have less than two hours to get ourselves together and out of here before we miss our flight," I told her, glancing over at the clock.

Her eyes followed mine and widened after seeing what time it was. "Ashley, it's almost three in the morning! What the hell are you talking about? Where are we going?"

"Jamaica." I shrugged.

Her face screwed up as she stared at me. "It's late, and I'm too tired to be playing with you, Ash. Move so I can go back to sleep."

"Okay, gon' back to sleep, but think it's a game if you want to. You gon' be around here looking crazy when I leave yo' ass," I told her, hopping up from the bed and moving to the closet so that I could pack me a quick bag.

It took me ten minutes flat to get my bag ready since I had only packed my necessities. I figured that anything else I needed, I could just get it there. Jordyn was still lying in the bed when I emerged from the closet, but her head popped up after hearing me drop my bag by the bedroom door.

"Ashley, where the hell are you going?"

"Girl, I just told yo' ass Jamaica. You thought I was lying?"

Realizing that I was indeed serious, she sprang from the bed with the speed of lightning and bolted past me. After rummaging through the closet, sifting through the little clothes that she'd managed to accumulate, she stomped back into the room with her lip poked out.

"What the hell am I supposed to pack? I don't have anything to wear in Jamaica."

"If your stubborn ass had let me take you shopping back when I offered, maybe you would." I shrugged. "Don't sweat it. We'll go shopping when we land. Just make sure you grab that toothbrush and handle that breath. Shit's a little tart, shorty."

"Shut up, rude ass. You came in here waking me up out of my sleep. Don't be expecting my shit to be minty fresh," she said, pushing me away from her. "Since you plan on blowing a few bags when we get there, I guess I'm good to go."

"Nah, you're not. I was dead ass about that breath, shorty. Handle that."

"Ugh. I can't stand you." She huffed and flipped me off before stomping her short ass into the bathroom.

"Yeah, whatever. Love you too. Now, chop chop, ma. We gotta be on the I-10 in ten."

࿐

MAN, IF I COULD DESCRIBE JAMAICA WITH ONE WORD, IT would be simply *beautiful*. I was still trying to figure out why I had never been there before now. Being in Jamaica had me finally realizing the true meaning of paradise. The place was something serious.

It was crazy how a sense of calm came over you the second you stepped foot on the island. Jordyn's behind had been like a kid in a candy store since the moment we touched down. I couldn't even blame her, and let her do her thing. We had only been there three days, and she had us out here doing some of everything.

Jordyn had my butt out there on some damn jet skis and even hit the dunes. I had to draw the line when she tried to talk me into swimming with some damn dolphins. She could have that. I'd be damned if I got in there with those big ass creatures. I wasn't scared or no shit like that, but they could stay over there in the water, and I'd be just fine here on land.

"Oh my God, Ash!" Jordyn exclaimed excitedly as she ran up on me. "Did you see that? One of them gave me a kiss! Why didn't you get in with me?"

"Because somebody had to take the pictures, baby." I laughed, tossing my arm across her shoulders. "But I'm glad you had fun. At least you made it out alive."

118

"You're so dramatic, Ashley. I don't think a doggone dolphin would have killed me," she said, rolling her eyes as she laughed.

"How you know that? Don't be underestimating them just because they look all cute and innocent and shit. Them mother-fuckers can still be dangerous."

"I don't believe this." She cracked up, shaking her head at me. "Big Bad Ash is scared of some damn dolphins."

Mushing her head away from me, I frowned down at her. "Ain't nobody scared, but let one of them had tried to bite your leg off. You'd be singing a different tune."

"I can't with you, Ashley. Bring your crazy behind on. I want ice-cream."

Hand in hand, we strolled down the beach after grabbing our frozen treats without a care in the world. From the outside looking in, you would never know that we had so much bullshit waiting for us when we returned home. None of it mattered while we were here. We were able to put our problems on hold and be in our own little bubble.

"You two are such a lovely couple," an older woman commented as she and her husband passed us. "Honeymoon?"

"Thank you," Jordyn said, blushing. "But no, ma'am. Just vacationing."

"Oh, I'm sorry. I just saw that glow and smile, and you two reminded me of my Earnest, and I when we first married. I figured you had to be newlyweds." She smiled at us. "Any who. Enjoy your vacation."

Jordyn politely waved, and I nodded my head to her and her husband as they went on their way. We fell back into step as we headed further away from our condo and down the beach. We had fallen into a comfortable silence, and I began to get lost in my thoughts.

"If I could stay here forever, I think I would. It's so beautiful out here," Jordyn said, gaining my attention. She stared out toward the water as the waves crashed up against the shore. "It almost seems fake."

Pulling her back to my front, I nuzzled my nose into her hair and inhaled her scent. "Nah, it's definitely real, ma. Hell, we don't have to leave. With the way I'm feeling, I'll hit my realtor up right now."

"Yeah, right. You can't just up and move to Jamaica."

"Yes, *we* can," I retorted.

"*We* definitely can't. What I look like just up and moving clean out the country? We got whole lives and families back home," she said. "Besides, Grams ain't raise no fool. You think I'm about to be moving out here, and you ain't put a ring on my finger? No, sir. I think not."

"Then, shit, let's do it."

"Do what?" she asked in confusion.

"You said you ain't moving out here if ain't no ring on your finger, so let's get married."

"Boy, quit playing with me," she said, waving me off.

She tried pulling my arm so that we could resume our walk, but I didn't budge. "Does it look like I'm playing?" I asked. "Let's get married, Jo. Right now."

"Are you serious? What is wrong with you, Ashley? Like really. First, you want to fly all the way to Jamaica out of nowhere. Now, you're talking about 'let's get married.' You're too young to be going through a midlife crisis."

"No, what I am is too damn impatient to be wasting time when I know what I want. Ma, this isn't just some random shit that popped in my head. Trust me. You know I don't even move like that. I thought this shit through. Jordyn, marriage ain't never been on the table for me until I met you. I *know* that I'm going to make you my wife one day, so why not make that day today?"

"Because we haven't been together long enough to be talking about marriage, Ashley. That's why. We still have so much to learn about each other, and we're still young," she said, shaking her head. "This is crazy."

"What's crazy is us sitting here doing this boyfriend-girlfriend bullshit when you could be my wife. We're going to be getting to know each other for the rest of our lives, and don't use that age excuse. Our age don't mean shit to me," I said, folding my arms across my chest. "I know what I want, Jo, and that's you. I don't need months or years of dating to figure that out. I can't even put into words how much I love your stubborn behind. The thought of us not being together makes me sick to my stomach, ma. I can't see myself with anyone else. I don't even want to entertain the idea. This is it for me, Jo. *You're* it for me."

Sniffling, she dabbed the corners of her eyes. "Since when did you become a sap?" she asked, laughing through her tears.

"Since the moment your little mean ass came barging into my life trying to shake shit up." I chuckled, pulling her into my arms.

After a few seconds of standing in each other's embrace, she pulled away and glanced up at me.

"Okay, Ashley."

"Okay? 'Okay' what?" I asked with a raised brow.

"Okay, let's do it. Let's get married."

I stared at her for a moment, trying to determine if she was serious. When her gaze didn't waver, I felt my pulse accelerate as adrenaline coursed through my veins. I wasn't expecting her to really be on board with it.

"Yo, you're serious? Like for real serious?" I asked anxiously.

Her eyes bucked. "Yes, I'm serious. Were you bullshitting with me, Ashley, because I swear, I'll—"

"Hell no," I said, grabbing her hand and hurriedly pulling her behind me. "Come on."

"Slow down," she giggled, trying to keep up with the strides of my longs legs. "Where are we going *now?*"

"To get you a ring and get married. Where else?"

12

MARCEL

Lightly tapping my fist against the slightly ajar door, I slowly pushed it open and allowed the bouquet of lilies to lead the way into the room. No one knew about it, but almost every day before I headed down to the shop I would stop by Grams' house to check in on her and just chill for a while. I was not sure why, because half the time, Grams was too medicated to even know that I was there.

When she did so happen to be alert, we had some of the best talks. Now, our talks had become one-sided with me doing most of the talking since her health was rapidly declining.

She took a liking to me too. I couldn't blame her, though. Who wouldn't love your boy?

"Hi, Mr. Marcel," her nurse chimed after noticing me enter the room.

Nurse Debbie had gotten used to seeing my face around and was cool about keeping my visits on the hush. Of course, I slid her a little something extra in exchange for her silence. I wasn't really trying to have Fatima all in my ear if she found out about me still visiting her mom after we parted ways. It honestly had nothing to do with her.

I had grown attached to Grams since the moment Fatima had first introduced us. It could have been because she reminded me so much of my own grandmother. They both were feisty as hell with the most genuine hearts. Whatever it was, Grams had earned a spot in my heart.

"Hey, beautiful." I smiled at Grams, placing the flowers by her bedside.

Her eyes were barely open, but I noticed that her lips creased upward as they struggled to form a smile after realizing that it was me. One of her hands slightly stretched in my direction, beckoning me to her. Taking the flowers from my hand, Nurse Debbie smiled at me as she inhaled their aroma.

"Honey, you keep bringing all these pretty flowers in here, and we're going to run out of room," she joshed, moving to find an empty space to place them on the dresser.

"Well, I was taught to give people their flowers while they're here," I said, kissing Grams' forehead. "How are we feeling today, young woman? You took your medicine this morning?"

"You see she's awake now, so that's a good thing. She's usually asleep by the time you get here. I haven't given her the pain meds just yet. She seems to be doing fine for now, so I figured I'd let you two have your morning talk first."

"'Preciate that, Nurse Deb. Have you been able to get her to eat anything?"

She sighed and shook her head. "No, not really. We tried the applesauce earlier. You know how she is, and she's been putting up a fight."

"Well, we know where her stubborn daughter and grand-daughter gets it from." I laughed, shaking my head and turning back to Grams. "OG, you can't be in here giving Nurse Deb a hard time. How you plan on getting better if you won't eat?"

Grams looked as if she wanted to say something, but before she could get a syllable out, violent coughs overtook her. I quickly moved to grab her the cup of water from beside her and pushed the straw toward her lips. After taking a few sips, she rested back against her pillows and squeezed her eyes shut.

"I'm going to go ahead and prepare her medicine," Nurse Debbie advised.

Making myself comfortable in the recliner next to Grams' bed, I relaxed in the chair as I focused my attention on the TV where an episode of *Golden Girls* was playing. I laughed to myself, remembering all the nights that Fatima and I would stay up bingeing on the show while we exchanged stories of our childhoods. I couldn't believe she had me watching it, but the craziest part was that I actually enjoyed it.

"What the hell are you doing here?"

Cursing under my breath, I momentarily closed my eyes before turning to face an angry Fatima. Even with the scowl plastered on her face, she was still beautiful as hell. All that sassiness didn't do anything but heighten her appeal.

Standing to my feet, I stretched my arms above my head and took my precious time acknowledging her. I turned to Grams and placed a kiss upon her forehead, making plans to stop by later that week.

"So you don't hear me? I asked what you're doing here," Fatima repeated.

"Well, I was trying to chill and watch TV until you came bringing your negative energy and attitude all up in here."

"Marcel, please don't play with me. Why are you at my mother's house? You stalking me or something?"

"Ma, don't flatter yourself. I wouldn't waste my time," I told her and noticed her mouth drop open at my bluntness before she quickly recovered. "I'm here to check on Grams. That's it. You got a problem with that?"

"As a matter of fact, I do," she stated, defiantly. "We aren't together anymore, Marcel. I don't need you popping in on my mama."

"What does us being together have to do with anything? So because we no longer mess with each other, that means I have to stop giving a damn about Grams' wellbeing? Ma, grow up," I told her.

"Whatever. I'm grown over here. What you need to do is let me worry about *my* mother's wellbeing, and you focus on that baby that you have on the way."

Chuckling, I shook my head as I headed for the door. "That bitter bit doesn't suit you, shorty. I'll concern myself with who and what I want. I'm sorry if you aren't mature enough to handle my presence. I'll try to do a better job of staying out your way," I told her and stopped before I could exit the room. "And for your information, I *don't* have a baby on the way. But you would know that already had you stuck around. You enjoy the rest of your day."

⚜

PATIENCE HAD NEVER BEEN MY STRONGEST TRAIT, AND I'D BE lying if I said I wasn't close to spazzing out. Heaven had been screaming to the top of her lungs for the last thirty minutes, and I was seconds away from blowing my own damn head off.

We had just gotten back from the emergency room, because I was scared that it was something seriously wrong with her. Heaven was a good baby, and I wasn't just saying that because she was mine. She was one of the most laid-back babies I knew, and it was completely out of the norm for her to be turning up on me like this.

Thankfully, the doctors were able to figure out what was wrong with her, and it turned out that she was only teething, which had led to an ear infection and fever. That only made me feel a little better, but it still messed me up that I couldn't do anything to take the pain away.

"Come on, Hev. Daddy's trying, baby," I said, rocking her back and forth in my arms.

I glanced down at my watch, trying to figure out when the medicine that the doctor had prescribed would kick in. Hell, we both needed to be getting some rest.

Trying to get to my ringing phone had me struggling to balance her in my arms as I searched through the clutter that had accumulated on the coffee table.

"Yo?" I answered, placing the call on speaker.

"Hey, Cel. How's my baby doing?" my mom inquired.

"You can still hear her, can't you?" I asked in frustration. "I already gave her the medicine, but it doesn't seem to be doing a damn thing. She's still burning the hell up."

"It takes a minute, baby. How long ago did you give it to her?"

"Like twenty minutes ago."

"You have to give it time, Cel. You sure you don't need me to come over? You know I will. My baby needs her Glam-ma to make her feel better."

"No, Ma." I sighed. "I can't keep calling you for everything."

"Well, technically, *I* called you."

"Ma, you know what the hell I mean. I depend on you enough as it is. Heaven is *my* child. I should be able to take care of her. This ain't no temporary or part-time shit. If I'm gon' do this for real, I'm gon' have to get used to nights like these. I can't run to you every time something is wrong. As her father, I should be able to handle a little fever. We got this over here."

"Well, excuse me. Just make sure that my baby know that granny got her if daddy don't know what he's doing over there," she said jokingly. "On a serious note, Cel. I want you to know that I'm really proud of you. What you're doing is not easy, but you're stepping up to the plate. Just know that you're not alone in this. You have a strong support system right behind you. Remember that."

Knock. Knock.

"I hear you, Ma. Hold on right quick. Somebody's at the door," I told her, moving to look out the peephole.

"Who the hell is that this late? My baby already not feeling well. You need to tell them they need to keep it moving, and come back some other time," she nagged.

My head jerked back, and my face frowned in confusion after seeing who was on the other side.

"Aye, Ma. I'll hit you later. Let me get this," I told her and hung up before she could get another word out.

I tossed the phone to the side and pulled the door open. "You lost or something?" I asked, peering down at my uninvited guest.

"Umm. No, I'm not lost, Marcel. Can I come in?" Fatima asked, looking everywhere but at me.

"For what? What's in here that you need?" I asked, shifting a fussy Heaven from one arm to the next.

"Really, Marcel?" She sighed. "Look, I just wanted to talk to you. I didn't realize that Heaven would still be awake."

"Well, as you can see, she is. We're a little busy right now, so say whatever it is that you need to say so that I can get back to tending to my child."

Fatima moved in closer as her eyes zeroed in on Heaven's small frame. "What's wrong with her? She's usually not this fussy."

"She's fine," I said, blowing her off and protectively turning Heaven away from her. "What's up?"

"Come on, Marcel. Is this really what we've come to? You

can't even let me in? Instead, I have to stand out here on your porch to talk to you."

"Ma, you're the one that made things like this between us. I'm not trying to make you uncomfortable or anything. Just the other day you were acting like being in my presence was going to kill you."

"That's what I came over to talk to you about. I wanted to apologize for how I acted toward you," she said, casting her eyes down toward her feet. "I was wrong for how I came at you. I know you've developed sort of a bond with my mom. I guess seeing you just threw me off. I wasn't expecting it. At first, I felt like you had other motives."

"What motives, Fatima? Unlike you, I'm not into playing games. I was there because I genuinely give a damn about your moms."

"And I know that, Marcel. Like I said, I wanted to apologize for how I came at you. It was out of line, and I really do appreciate you for being there for my mother," she said, finally making eye contact with me.

"Man, that's nothing. I wasn't doing it for a pat on the back," I told her. "Is that all you wanted?"

"Damn. I guess it is," she replied sadly and slowly turned to retreat back to her car.

Even though I had just curved the hell out of her, I wasn't a complete asshole. I waited until she made it all the way inside her car, which took her forever, before I closed and locked my door. She was taking her sweet precious time like there was a chance that I would change my mind and stop her. *Not!*

Like I had told Ash, I was done playing games with Fatima, and I'd be damned if I chased her. Besides, the only reason she came over here with that bullshit apology was because of the bomb I'd dropped on her about Mariah not being pregnant with my seed. I was surprised that Jordyn hadn't already spilled the beans to her.

Either way, she could stay where she was at. I didn't need her up and dipping out on me anytime shit got rough. I had a child to think about, and Fatima wasn't being fair to either of us. The same way I had grown attached to Fatima, so had my baby girl. Fatima couldn't just be coming and going as she pleased. Heaven and I didn't need that type of inconsistency in our lives.

RING. RING. RING.

"Ughh!!" I groaned, roughly throwing the comforter from over my head.

Glancing over at the clock on my nightstand, I realized that I hadn't even been asleep for a good two hours. After dealing with a fussy Heaven all night, all I wanted to do was get some rest, but it didn't seem like that was happening.

13

JORDYN

Waking up, I was sure that I was going to discover that yesterday had all been a dream, but the huge rock that rested on my finger was saying otherwise. I still couldn't believe that Ash and I had really gotten married. What the hell were we thinking?

After seeing that the space beside me was empty, I figured that Ash was somewhere freaking out just like I was. He had to be having second thoughts too. I mean, who just randomly ups and gets married? Obviously, our crazy asses. I was just going to blame our irrational behavior on the allure of the island. That had to be it.

Feeling myself about to go into a full-on panic, I tossed the covers from over me and was about to climb out the bed, but the bedroom door being pushed open stopped me.

"Morning, beautiful. I see you finally rose from your coma." Ash smiled as he approached the bed and leaned down to kiss my lips. "How'd you sleep?"

"Umm, good," I cautiously answered. "How long have you been up?"

"I don't know." He shrugged. "A few hours. I couldn't sleep."

I fiddled with my fingers as my gaze dropped. "Are you having regrets?"

"Regrets about what?"

"About this, Ashley," I said, flashing my ring in his face. "What else?"

"Hell, I don't know," he said, shrugging. "You could have been talking about anything. I don't have a reason why you would even think I would have *any* regrets about that. You better not be having any either."

"I don't know what I'm feeling, Ashley. We really got married. Like... *really*," I told him. "You have to be a little on edge about that. That's probably the reason you're restless."

"No, I couldn't sleep because I was too damn excited and didn't want to wake you. You needed your rest after last night. That husband dick had you laid out."

"*Husband dick?*" I fell out laughing. "What the hell is that, Ashley?"

"Exactly what I put on yo' ass last night," he answered cockily. "In here crying and shit, speaking in tongues like you were about to be sent to glory."

"Shut up," I shrieked, hiding my face in embarrassment. "I was *not* crying."

"You calling me a liar?" He challenged me, inching closer to the bed with a mischievous smirk on his face.

"No, babe," I quickly answered, looking for an escape.

"Nah, I think you were," he said and pounced on me before I could think.

"Ash, wait. Babe, you're squishing me." I giggled uncontrollably. "You're trying to change the subject too."

Still trapping me against the bed, he adjusted his weight and held himself up by his forearms. His lustful glare bore into me, and I knew that I was in trouble. Good trouble, though. *Very* good trouble.

"What subject?"

"The subject of whether you're sure we made the right move," I told him, staring into his intense eyes.

"Listen, shorty, I can't speak for you, but I did exactly what I wanted to do. Nothing in me regrets making you *Mrs.* Ashley Thomas. I'd marry you every day for the rest of my life if that's what I needed to do to show you that I'm serious about this shit."

Lowering his face until our lips were only a breath apart, Ash's tongue darted out from in between his plump lips and swiped teasingly across my mouth. A moan slipped from between my lips, and my hips involuntarily thrust upward into his pelvis. It only took the slightest touch for that man to have me coming completely undone.

"Is that what you need me to do, Jo-Jo?" he asked closer to my ear. "Huh?"

I allowed my eyes to drift closed as he began a trial of kisses starting at my mouth and making his way to my neck and down between my breasts. My fingers glided through his hair, caressing his scalp as he worshipped my body.

After methodically licking almost every inch of me, his head found its way between my legs. Before I could brace myself, he had already began his assault on my clit, granting me zero mercy.

"Ashley! Baby, wait," I cried out in ecstasy, trying to escape his monster tongue.

"What am I waiting for? Move your hand," he ordered, slapping my hand away from where I was pushing against his head.

Draping my thighs across his shoulders, he sat up on his knees, leaving my shoulders and head resting on the bed. Ash sat there and ate me like I was a full course meal and was still at it like he was searching for dessert.

The entire time he was buried between my legs, his phone had been ringing off the hook, but not once did his concentration break. He was determined to find whatever treasure his tongue was digging for in my kitty. I was in no way prepared when my orgasm snuck up on me, and I released onto his tongue. He eagerly lapped up my juices, using his tongue to clean up the mess he made.

"Damn, shorty. You taste good as fuck." He smiled down at me as he lowered me back to the bed. "Spread them legs open for me, baby."

His hard body settled between my thighs, and I moaned loudly at the feeling of him stroking his thick erection against my clit. I was trying to focus on the feeling of intense ecstasy that was consuming my entire body, but his phone was really starting to irk my nerves. I could barely concentrate on my nut.

"Baby, can you please get that, or turn it off?" I pouted. "Whoever it is has been blowing you up."

"Forget that phone. *This* is the only thing that you should be worried about," he said right as he was slipping inside of me.

My breath caught in my throat, and I could have sworn I saw stars. No matter how many times Ash and I were intimate, every time he entered me felt like the first time.

"This the only thing that needs to be on your mind," he said, stroking me expertly. "Ain't that right?"

"Yes! Yes, baby," I cried out, gripping his shoulders as he pushed deeper, his hips meeting mine. "Oh God, yes! I'm about to cum!"

"Already?" he asked arrogantly, smirking down at me. "That was too easy, baby girl."

"Be quie—Oh fuuuuck! Please, don't stop! Right there!" I screamed, unable to control myself.

I was almost certain that just about everyone on our floor could hear me with how loud he had me in here screaming. Ash always put it down in the bedroom, but it was like us being married unlocked a whole new level of dick. I wasn't prepared for it.

I had lost count of how many rounds we went at it and the numerous orgasms we both shared. All I knew was that every muscle in my body ached by the time Ash was done with me.

Whatever energy I *thought* I had was wiped away, and I was ready to go right back to sleep. I needed to regroup and get myself together if I was going to be able to make it out the bed.

Ring. Ring. Ring.

My head shot up from where it rested on Ash's chest, and I frowned at the sound of his phone going off yet again.

"Okay, seriously, Ash. You need to get that," I told him.

"Man, I'm trying to enjoy my vacation," he grumbled. "I told everybody not to be calling me."

"Which is exactly why you need to answer. It could be something serious."

Deciding that I was right, he snatched his phone from the table, and his eyes squinted at the screen.

"It's Cello," he announced before answering. "Bruh, why you blowing me up? I'm trying to spend time with my wife. What's good?"

I sat beside Ash, looking on as he listened to whatever Marcel was telling him. His face wasn't giving away much, but from the way his body tensed up, I knew Marcel couldn't have been giving him good news. His eyes cast over to me while his face held a somber expression.

"Yeah, man. I'm about to see what I can do now. I'll hit you back when I find something out," Ash told him before disconnecting the call.

"What was that about, babe?"

He ignored me for a minute, before finally turning to me. "Baby, I need you to get dressed for me, and go pack up our things. We have to go."

"Go? Why? Tell me what's going on, Ash. Is everything alright? What did Cello want?"

"Jordyn, baby, I just need you to do what I said, okay?" he asked and got up from the bed, grabbing his basketball shorts along the way. "Go pack, and just let me worry about everything else. I'm about to see if I can find us a flight."

"Ash, you're scaring me. I'm not about to do anything until you tell me *something*. What did he say?" I asked, standing to my feet as well but not bothering with any clothes. "It had to be something serious if we're cutting our trip short."

Coming over and taking both of my hands in his, he looked down at me with sad eyes. "Sit down for me, baby."

"No, Ashley. Tell me," I demanded, defiantly.

"It's Grams, Jo."

෴

I HAD NO IDEA WHEN WE LEFT THE RESORT. I HAD NO IDEA when we boarded a plane. I had no idea when we finally made it back to the states. I had no idea when we loaded into the car that was waiting for us. The only time I checked into reality was when we turned into my grandmother's neighborhood and pulled into the driveway. I was stuck in a trance as I sat frozen with tears streaming down my face.

I thought that I was ready for it, but I wasn't. I wasn't ready to say goodbye. I couldn't.

"Jo," Ash called out softly, grabbing my hand and intertwining our fingers. "Come on, mama. We have to go inside."

"I'm not ready, Ash. I can't do this," I said, shaking my head frantically.

"Baby, look at me," Ash said, turning me to face him. "Yes, you can do this, Jo. You have to. Faye needs you, ma, and *you* need this. That shit will eat at you if you don't get the chance to say goodbye. Trust me, I know. Come on. Grams is waiting for you. I got you, shorty. I keep telling you that you're not in this alone."

"I know, babe." I nodded, squeezing his hand. "I'm ready."

He brought my wedding ring up to his lips and kissed it. "Let's get inside."

Hand in hand, we walked inside, and I felt my legs growing weak with every step I took. Seemingly noticing my struggle, Ash pulled me protectively into his side, supporting my weight. The first face I saw was my mother's when we entered through the front door.

"Jordyn," she said, hopping to her feet and coming to me but my hand flew up, stopping her.

"Not today, Constance. I'm here for my grandmother, and that's it," I told her coldly.

"Listen, I know you feel however you feel about me, and I don't give a damn, but—"

"Aye, back up for me," Ash said, stepping in between us and squaring his shoulders.

Ash might not have seen my mother to know who she was, but I was sure from the countless stories I'd shared with him that he was able to put two and two together.

"Whatever beef y'all might have is irrelevant. Now is not the time. Y'all can handle that shit later, but for now, you're about to get out of her face. Let her see her grandmother like she came here to do."

She reared back in shock that Ash had come at her like that, but I wasn't surprised at all. Ash was extremely protective of those he cared about.

"Who the hell—"

"Jordyn!"

Fatima rushed into the room and straight for me, rushing into my arms.

"Faye," I instantly cried out. "How is she?"

"Bad." She bawled. "I'm losing my mama, Jo! She's leaving us!"

"I know, Faye. I know." I broke down with her.

We stayed in the same spot wrapped in each other's arms for what felt like hours, neither of us wanting to pull away. It wasn't until Ash walked over to us and wrapped his arms around our shoulders, ushering us toward Grams' room, that we pulled away to look at him.

Anxiety overtook me, and I was ready to turn away and flee from the house, but Ash held me firm and shook his head. "I got you, Jordyn. You can't keep running."

As always, he just had to be right. Nodding in agreement, I grabbed Fatima's hand in mine and faced Grams' door. I took a deep breath before twisting the knob and pushing it open.

The person in front of me was not the person I knew to be my grandmother. It had only been a little over a week since I last saw Grams, and there was a huge change in her appearance. She had already been losing enough weight as it was, but now she appeared to be only skin and bones.

Nurse Debbie smiled sympathetically at me as I inched closer to Grams' bedside. Tears blinded my vision as I gazed down at her frail frame.

"Look who's here to see you," Nurse Debbie announced to Grams.

Grams' eyes were closed, but I knew from the constant moaning that she was doing that she wasn't sleeping. The pain she was experiencing was stopping her from getting any rest.

Taking her fragile hand in mine, I bent down to place a kiss on the back of it and almost immediately felt tears begin to cascade down my cheeks.

"Hey, Grams," I said just above a whisper.

I moved to climb into the small hospital bed that they had replaced her normal bed with and gently rested my head on her shoulder.

"I missed you. Ash and I just got back from Jamaica," I told her, stroking her hair. "Man, Grams, I wish you could have seen how beautiful it was out there. Everything was almost *too* perfect. If I wasn't already so chocolate, I would have definitely had a pretty bad tan. Ash could barely get me to come out of the water."

I had lost track of the hours that I lay there talking to my grandmother about everything under the sun. Everyone had been trying to get me to move from the bed and step out to get some fresh air, but I wasn't having it. I planned on staying right in that room for as long as I needed to.

Ash and Marcel had even pulled a couple of extra chairs into the room. I was not sure how it came about, but before I knew it, a game of Spades had broken out. For the first time since I walked into the house, I was able to genuinely smile and laugh. I had to say a quick 'thank you' to the man upstairs for placing Ash and Marcel into my and Fatima's lives. They were doing everything in their powers to make sure that we were okay, even if that meant only providing a temporary distraction.

"Give me that, playboy," Ash said to Marcel, beckoning the cards his way. "My baby got that."

"Man, y'all some cheaters. Y'all be doing all that slick talking across the table, but I peep game," Marcel quipped, flinging the book of cards toward Ash playfully.

"Cello, you always swear somebody cheating." I laughed, playing my next card. "Just take this whooping like you always do."

"See, Jordyn, we were just getting back cool, but I'm starting not you like you anymore."

"Yeah, yeah, whatever. Play your card, so I can go 'head and get that up off ya," I taunted.

"You make me sick, midget," he grumbled, tossing his card out. "I bet—"

The bedroom door flung open, and Constance stood there in the doorway with her nose turned up. "So y'all just in here having a whole party while my mother is over there lying on her deathbed."

"Constance, don't come in here with your bullshit," Fatima snapped irritably. "We're in here minding our business. *My* mama is just fine."

"Lil' girl, that was *my* mama way before you were even thought about," she said, waving Fatima off. "And don't forget who the hell *your* big sister is."

"What I *am* about to forget is that I have any sense. Why must you come messing with us? We were good in here, and y'all were good out there."

"I can go wherever I please in my mother's house. You don't—"

"You sure are throwing that 'my mother' bit around a lot. Now that she's dying, you want to come around," Fatima growled. "Where were you when she needed a way to all of her appointments? Where were you when she got so sick that she could barely feed herself, let alone wipe her own ass? Where were you when we had to figure out how we were going to afford all this expensive ass medicine and shit? Where were you, Constance? Because it damn sure wasn't here. You only came around when you needed something or were in some trouble that you needed Mama to get you out of. Instead of being a good daughter and mother, yo' doped out ass was too busy chasing your next high. You could have stayed wherever the hell you were at."

Well, damn. Fatima usually didn't have much of anything to say to Constance, but she'd said more than a mouthful then. I guess she had finally reached her wits end with her, and I didn't blame Fatima. Constance just had that type of effect on people.

"Little bitch! You—"

Constance made a move in Fatima's direction, but was unsuccessful as Ash and Marcel both hopped to their feet at the same time.

"We not doing that," Ash said calmly.

Constance was a lot of things, including stupid, but I guess she chose that moment to at least pretend like she had a lick of sense. She knew just like everyone else in this room that there was no way in hell she was going to make it through those two big ass men to get to Fatima. Even in the event that she did, she would have most definitely gotten jumped in here. I already owed her bigtime and would have gladly stomped a hole in her ass. She did right to back down.

After receiving an instant migraine, courtesy of Constance, I had sort of zoned out and didn't even realize that I had dozed off on them until I felt myself being shaken awake.

"What?" I groaned, sleepily.

"Jordyn, wake up," Fatima said, shaking me again.

When I finally opened my eyes, I realized that everyone was standing around Grams' bedroom with somber looks on their face, including Constance and my uncle Henry. Already knowing what that meant, I squeezed my eyes shut in an attempt to gather myself before I was forced to face the inevitable. My eyes welled with tears as the sound of Grams agonizing moans of pain filled the room.

"We need to give her more of the meds, Faye. She's hurting,"

I told Fatima, not understanding why they were all just standing around doing nothing.

Fatima responded by shaking her head as she too shed tears. "She's already had enough of the pain meds, Jo. We can't just keep her drugged up," she told me, stroking Grams' head in a soothing motion. "Jo, we're going to take her off the oxygen."

"For what? You heard Nurse Debbie say that was what was keeping her—" I stopped mid-sentence as my eyes widened. My fists clenched at my side as I violently shook my head in opposition. "No, Faye. No, we're not doing that. Just give her the medicine so that she can sleep."

"No, Jordyn," Fatima stated firmly. "We have to. I don't want this to happen just as much as you don't, but look at her, Jordyn. She's in pain and miserable, and there's nothing we can do about it. I can't keep seeing her like this. It's selfish of us to try to keep her here with us when we both know it's time for her to go."

"Please, no, Faye," I cried out weakly, feeling my knees buckle.

Ash was right at my side, supporting me just like he had been through this entire thing. He pulled me into his chest and rested his chin atop my head.

"Listen to me, baby," he said. "I know you're not ready for this, but you know this is what Grams would want. She's suffering, Jo. We can't keep holding her here. It's her time, ma, and she's already let you know that she was at peace with it. She lived her life, baby, and she's done everything she's set out to do while she was here on this earth with us. She's fought for as long as she could, baby. It's time for her body to get some rest."

"I know." I sobbed into his chest. "I know."

"Then tell her that," Ash said, pulling away slightly so that he could look into my eyes. "You know your grandmother is not going anywhere until she knows her babies are okay. That's that stubbornness," he said jokingly. "Talk to her, Jo. Give her that peace."

Nodding my head, I squeezed my arms around Ash's torso, trying to gather as much of his strength as I could before I pulled away and went to kneel beside Grams' bed.

"Hey, babe." I sniffled, smiling at Grams weakly as I continuously stroked her hair. Closing my eyes, I took a deep breath before I continued. "I hate seeing you like this. I know you've been trying to hold on for us as long as you could, and you've put up a good fight. You've been sooo strong, Grams."

I felt Fatima grip my hand and squeeze it after hearing my voice crack as I tried my best to remain strong.

"So strong," I continued, allowing my tears to fall freely as I rested my head on her chest. "But it's time for you to rest, baby. It's going to be okay. *We're* going to be okay. You don't have to be strong anymore. You don't have to feel this pain anymore. Rest, G. We'll see you on the other side. Just be sure to save a spot for us up there with you."

I stayed in that same position, listening to the faint sound of her heartbeat until I could no longer hear it. I knew that I'd told Grams that we would be okay, but the second that last breath left her body, I felt my heart breaking into a million pieces, and I lost it. What was I going to do without my heart?

14

ASH

I had been around death my whole life, and it had become almost an everyday encounter for me. The last time that I could righteously say that someone's passing affected me was when I lost my mom. Other than that, I was almost immune to feeling emotions toward it. That was until I had to sit there and hold an inconsolable Jordyn in my arms as her heart ached for her grandmother.

I felt helpless as I watched her disintegrate right before my eyes. I thought the death of my mother broke me, but it was something completely different watching Jordyn and Fatima become so undone. I had to shed a few tears of my own.

"Jo," I called out, stepping into Grams' room.

Jordyn and Fatima were curled up in the middle of Grams' bed, exactly where they had been since the coroner came and picked up the body. They refused to eat anything, and it was impossible to get them to leave the room or the house.

I was grateful that Grams had taken it upon herself to get all of her arrangements in order and handled most of that business ahead of time, or we'd be messed up. Neither one of the ladies were in the mind space to do anything.

"Baby," I called out again since she ignored me the first time. "Come on, mama. I need for you and Faye to get yourselves together. It's about time for us to be leaving. The driver called, and the cars should be here in the next thirty minutes."

"I don't want to go, Ash. Can't I just stay here?" Jordyn whined, wrapping her arms around her body and visibly shaking. "I don't feel well. I can already feel myself getting sick."

"No, you can't stay here. You're just nervous and anxious. That's why you're feeling sick," I told her, swinging her legs from the bed and carefully planting her feet on the floor. "Ma, look at your dress, man. You wrinkled it up by laying in that bed. Get up, bae. You need to get up too, Faye. Come on. Everybody's waiting on you two. Y'all got ten minutes."

After leaving Jordyn and Fatima alone to get themselves together, I almost thought I was going to have to go back in that room and drag them out. Right before I was about to get up again, they came slowly strolling down the hallway hand in hand.

"Right on time," Marcel commented, standing at the window and announcing the arrival of our cars.

"Ready?" I asked with a raised brow as I looked between Jordyn and Fatima.

"Ready as we're gonna be," Fatima answered, clasping Jordyn's hand tighter and extending her free one out for Marcel to take.

⚜

PULLING UP TO GRAMS' HOUSE, I CUT MY ENGINE AND released a harsh breath. I already knew what I was about to face when I walked back in this house. I had only been gone for a couple of hours to handle some business, but Marcel had already informed that the ladies where still in the exact same spot as when I left.

It had been three whole days since we laid Grams to rest, and Jordyn and Fatima were still taking it pretty hard. Marcel and I had barely left their sides at all. I was trying to do any and everything I could think of to bring them out of their funk, but nothing was working. It was time for a different approach, because I needed my Jordyn back.

"Hey, baby," I said, entering Grams' bedroom. "Get up for me, ma. We got some food up front for y'all."

"Ashley, I already told you that I don't have an appetite."

I understood that she was mourning, but I couldn't allow her to keep herself holed up in this room. I wasn't trying to be funny or anything, but shit was starting to get a little rank in here.

"Well, you better find one. You haven't eaten in the last two days. Hell, almost three, because one damn banana doesn't count. Don't play with me, Jordyn. You're about to eat even if I have to force feed you myself," I stated matter-of-factly. "I can't have you in here getting sick on me, baby. You have to take care of yourself... both of y'all. Y'all know Grams wouldn't even be having this, and she would be ready to get on *my* ass for not taking care of her girls."

"But—"

"Please, Jo," I pleaded, softening my tone. "Just try for me. You know your little greedy butt is starving. Cello's moms cooked and brought food over because I let her know y'all stubborn behinds wouldn't eat."

"She's here?" Fatima sat up and spoke for the first time.

"Yeah, she's up there with everyone else. She wanted to come and check on you guys, but I told her I wasn't sure if y'all were up to it," I told them.

"Umm. You can tell her she can come back," Faye told me.

Figuring that was a good sign, I hurried from the room in search of Ma Dukes and brought her back to the room with the girls. Seeing that they hadn't been up for company at all, I took this as a good sign.

"Hey, babies," Marcel's mom greeted them as she slowly entered the room. "How are you ladies holding up?"

"Not good." Fatima sniffled, falling into Ma Dukes' arms and allowing her to cradle her against her chest. "This hurts so bad."

"I know it does, baby," Ma Dukes said, rocking her. "I know this pain you're feeling seems like it's unbearable, but you two young ladies are strong. You are two of the strongest women I've ever met. I didn't get the opportunity to meet your mother while she was here with us, but just from the way you two talked about her, I know she was something special, and I know y'all got that strength from her. It's time to put it to use."

"How?" Fatima cried. "I don't know what to do, Ma. I don't even know where to start."

"Baby, you start by getting up out of this room and getting yourself together. Both of you," she said, looking in Jordyn's direction as well. "Come on. Get up. You girls go get yourselves freshened up, and come out here and eat."

Unlike the thousand and one times that I'd attempted to get them out of this room, they listened to Ma Dukes and got up. Wasn't that some mess? If I had known that that was all it took, I would have been called her over a long time ago.

We all sat around until they both finally emerged from the back of the house and joined us. The pain was still visible in their eyes, and I knew they were hurting, but at least we were taking steps in the right direction.

Patting my knee, I beckoned Jordyn over to me. I peeped the blush that she tried to hide as she slowly approached me and took a seat.

"Feeling better?" I asked, placing a quick peck to her lips.

She nodded and rested her head against my shoulder. "A little."

"Good. Your breath is smelling better too," I said jokingly, causing her to smack my arm.

"You better leave her alone," Ma Dukes said, coming over and handing Jordyn a plate of food. "Here, baby. I wasn't sure what you wanted, so I fixed you a little of everything."

My mouth instantly watered after glancing down at the plate she placed in front of us. "Where's mine, Ma?"

"In the kitchen, waiting on you to fix it," she answered.

"That's cold, Ma." I chuckled, shaking my head. "It's cool. My baby'll share with me."

"No, your baby won't," Jordyn replied with a mouth full of food. "Sorry, but you're going to have to get your own."

"Woooow," I replied in astonishment. "Two seconds ago, your big-headed ass wasn't even hungry. I see how you do, Jo. Remember that."

She shrugged and kept right along eating. Even though it was messed up that she couldn't even share with your boy, I wasn't complaining. I was just glad that she was finally eating.

"Have you two handled all of her affairs and business?" Ma Dukes asked them.

"Yes, ma'am," Fatima answered. "Mama made sure that just about everything was already handled. There's not much left for us to do."

"Well, that's good. That's less stress on you two."

"Yeah, it is. We were able to get mostly everything done before the funeral. Now we're waiting on the insurance companies. She had two separate policies in place. We should be able to pay off the house and everything with that."

"And even if it wasn't, you know that would already be taken care of," I chimed in and assured them.

"I know, Ash, and thank—"

"Hold on. Why the hell are y'all sitting here discussing my mama's business with these folks?" Constance butt in from across the room, interrupting Fatima. "It's none of their damn business. Why are they even here in the first place?"

"No, the better question is... why are you still here?" Fatima nastily replied. "You're worried about them in our business, but not once has your ass even volunteered to help with anything! Miss me with your bullshit. I swear you can get it today, and not one motherfucker in here is going to stop me from beating your ass."

Fatima usually wasn't really the one to turn up so quick, but I was starting to realize that being around Jordyn's mom brought out the worst in her. She really despised the woman.

"Fatima, sweetie, calm down. Don't let her get you worked up like this," Ma Dukes said, trying to get her to chill out.

"I'm sorry, Ma, but I'm tired of letting her slide. The only thing saving her from me going upside her head before was my mama. She's not here now, so I have zero tolerance for her crap," Fatima quipped. "I don't even know why she's still here. You never came around this much when Mama was alive."

"I'm about tired of you thinking you can come at me crazy!" Constance yelled, shooting to her feet. "Don't worry about why I'm around. I can be here if I want to. This is my mama's house."

"Nah. Correction, boo. This is *my* house," Fatima said, standing to her feet as well.

"The hell it is," their uncle said for the first time.

That nigga had been so quiet that I almost forgot he was even there. He never really said much of anything when I was around, and that was probably best. Jordyn had already filled me in on how much of a bitch he was.

"You don't even live here. How the hell you just gon' come up in here claiming shit?" their uncle quipped.

"Honey, I can claim it because my name's on it. Mama made sure of that." Fatima smirked, folding her arms across her chest.

"You a damn lie! My mama ain't put your name on shit!" Constance yelled, approaching Fatima swiftly.

"Constance, you bring your ass over here, and shit gon' be different," Fatima advised, standing her ground.

By then, Jordyn had stopped eating and stood as well. I was done with all the back and forth. That shit was starting to give me a headache. Jordyn's family had more drama than *Jerry Springer*.

"Aye, y'all chill out, man," I told them, taking my place in between them before they could get anywhere near each other. "Look, y'all got a lot of business that obviously needs to be handled with a damn lawyer present. Trying to fight each other every two seconds ain't gon' solve shit. Constance, go back over to your little corner. Faye, y'all sit down somewhere."

I knew it was about to be some shit when Constance scoffed and eyeballed me up and down with her lip turned up.

"Look, I don't know who the hell you *think* you are, but you better get the hell out my face. I let you slide earlier, but you don't know me," Constance barked at me, pointing her finger in my face. "Just because you're sleeping with one of those little sluts over there doesn't give you the right to hop your ass in shit that doesn't concern you. This is a family matter."

God as my witness, I was trying my best to remain calm, but she was pushing it being in my face. There I was, trying to be the peacemaker, and she was still trying to bring the savage out. Just as I was about to give her old ass the business, Jordyn stepped up and got in her face.

"And he *is* family. This man has done more for me and *your* mother in the short time that he's known us than you've done in your entire pathetic ass life," she growled at her. "Don't bring your ass in here starting shit. Oh, and you disrespect him again, and you won't have to worry about Faye. I'm gon' beat your junkie ass myself."

"You disrespectful lil' hoe! I birthed you! I'll kill you in here if you think I'm about to let you talk to me like that!" she yelled at Jordyn.

Calmly, I grabbed Jordyn's arm and pulled her back toward her seat. "Aye, Jo. Sit down," I instructed her and cast her a glance that dared her to defy me.

Turning back toward her moms, I slowly approached her, stalking her like a lion would its prey. My hard eyes bore down into her scared ones, and I knew without a doubt that I had her shook. After all that talking she was just doing, I didn't hear a peep as I backed her into the wall.

"I play about a lot of things," I stated. My deep voice was low and filled with authority. "But you see that woman sitting over there? She isn't one of them. You threaten my wife again and we gon' have a problem. I know for a *fact* you know who the fuck I am, and all those rumors you've heard about me are definitely true. It's nothing for me to end your life and not think twice about it. Trust me. Your best bet is to take your ass back where you were, and don't come back over here unless necessary. Do you understand me?"

Rolling her eyes, she attempted to move around me, but I blocked her path and bent down until we were face to face.

"That was a question that required an answer."

Reluctantly, she folded her arms across her chest and nodded her head. "Understood."

Without another word, I stepped away and allowed her to move before going to resume my seat as if nothing happened. Everyone sat staring at me as I picked Jordyn's fork up and scooped some of the food into my mouth.

"You ice cold, bruh," Marcel said, breaking the silence in the room. "You in here turning up on folks' mamas and shit. Then gon' sit here like you ain't did anything."

"Because I didn't. You know that wasn't turning up," I said, cutting my eyes over at Marcel.

"Nah, forget all that," Fatima said, waving us both off and tucking her arms under her breasts. "We need to bring it all the way back for a minute. I know like hell I'm not the only one that caught the whole '*my wife*' thing."

Hearing her say that, my eyes cut over to Jordyn, and I watched as she automatically tucked her hand between her thighs and looked away. Leave it to Fatima's nosy ass to point out my slip-up. Out of everything I had just said, that was the one thing that stuck out to her. Jordyn and I weren't necessarily trying to hide anything, but we hadn't had the opportunity to discuss how we planned on breaking the news to everyone.

I had to avoid eye contact because I wasn't going to be the one to spill the beans. I'd let Jordyn have the honor of doing that. Hell, one look at her and you wouldn't even have to ask. It was all over her face.

"Jordyn?" Fatima called out.

"Yeah, Faye?"

"Girl, don't 'yeah, Faye' me. You got something you need to be telling me?"

Figuring that we couldn't keep it a secret forever, Jordyn uncovered her hand and held it up so that they could see the ring.

"Maybe," she answered sheepishly.

"Oh my God, Jordyn!" Fatima exclaimed excitedly. "I can't believe it. How do you up and get engaged and not tell me?"

"Married actually. You're looking at Mrs. Ashley Thomas now," Jordyn proudly proclaimed.

"Oh, lord," Ma Dukes happily exclaimed. "Y'all damn children are taking me too fast. Ashley, I should choke your big behind in here. How you just gon' hop and get married without telling anybody?"

"It happened fast, ma. We really didn't plan anything. We just did it," I said, shrugging.

"Well, prepare your ass to *just do it* all over again. I know like hell you didn't think I was going to let this slide," Ma Dukes said, wagging her finger in my face. "We're doing this up the right way."

"The right way is whatever way ended with this woman being my wife. All that extra is irrelevant," I said, pulling Jordyn to me and onto my lap. "Ain't that right, baby?"

Ma Dukes waved the both of us off. "All that lovey-dovey mess is all fine and dandy, but we're still having a wedding, and I don't want to hear a word about it. I already never thought I'd see the day either of you boys ever settled down, let alone got married. Don't take this moment from me, Ashley."

"Man, congrats, bruh," Marcel told me, pulling me into a brotherly hug. "But I'm with Ma Dukes on this one. Nigga, I should beat yo' ass. How y'all just gon' sneak off when I was supposed to be the damn best man?"

"You know I got y'all, man. Plus, everybody know Jo's spoiled behind not going to let me off the hook that easily." I smirked, cutting my eyes at Jordyn. "She was already on my ass about us getting hitched. Trust me. Y'all gon' get y'all wedding. I'll leave all the planning shit to you women. Just tell me a time and place, and I'll be there with bells on."

"Aye, since y'all already married and whatnot, does that mean I can't throw my boy a bachelor party?" Marcel asked, grinning mischievously at Jordyn.

"Hell no."

"Hell yeah," Jordyn answered simultaneously.

I chuckled and shook my head. "Why I can't have a bachelor party, ma?"

"Because last I checked, you weren't a damn bachelor," she sassily replied.

"Aw, man. Come on, Jo-Jo. Let my boy be great. I've been planning this shit out in my head since that day you cussed his butt out down at the shop for snapping on you," Marcel joshed. "I knew he was going to wife your lil' crazy ass."

"Bruh, whatever." I laughed. "You didn't know a damn thing then and still don't now."

"But I see y'all married, though." Marcel smirked. "Now, as soon as she pops out one of your big-head babies, I'll be two for two."

"Babies?" Jordyn repeated, almost choking on nothing. "Hold on, playa. We—"

"We're working on it," I said, cutting her off.

Jordyn's brow raised as she glanced at me quizzically. I knew that I had thrown her off with that one. Other than the whole abortion situation a few months ago, we had never really discussed kids. Even when that occurred, I was even surprised by how upset I was by the whole thing.

Figuring that this was a conversation that needed to be had in private, I decided not to say anything else. I'm sure Jordyn was glad when they changed the subject and moved on to something less nerve-wrecking.

"Well, listen, babies. I'm about to get out of here," Ma Dukes announced. "My grandbabies are probably missing their Glam-ma by now. Cel, my juicy mama is staying with me tonight, right?"

"I mean, I did plan on grabbing her from Shan once I left here."

"Well, how about you not plan on it. We need our girls' time. We'll see you tomorrow," she said, kissing his cheek and patting him on the chest before moving over to me and leaning in to hug me. "Your mom would be so proud of the man you've become, Ashley. Don't hesitate to call me for *anything*. I'll see you all later."

The mention of my mom caused my throat to tighten, but I quickly shook the feeling off. Ma Dukes was right, though. I knew my OG was smiling down from ear to ear at me. I knew I was not a perfect nigga, but I strived to be the best that I could be. She had to be proud.

15

MARCEL

Rolling over in my bed, my arm automatically stretched blindly under the covers until I'd found my intended target. Securing my grip, I pulled the warm body close to mine and rested my chin atop their head.

"The sun's barely up yet, so why are you?" I questioned groggily.

"I don't know. Not really tired."

I peeked through one of my eyelids and looked down at Fatima. She tried to hide her face in my chest, but I had already caught a glimpse of her swollen red eyes. It was evidence that she had spent a majority of her night crying.

"Ma, have you even been to sleep?"

"No," she answered, sniffling. "I can't. Every time I close my eyes, all I see is my mama laying there. I can't get that out my head, Cel. It won't go away."

"It's okay, baby," I said, attempting to soothe her. "Everything's still fresh, Faye. Things aren't going to get better overnight, but you have to know that it *does* get better. It just takes time, baby girl."

"I know. I just feel so stuck. Like, I don't know what I'm going to do. I feel like my entire world has been shaken. All I had were my mama and Jordyn. My mama is gone, and Jordyn has her own life to live. I'm happy for her and proud, but now, it's just me. I'm alone."

"Look, I don't want to ever hear you say that, Fatima. You're never *alone*. I don't care what Jo and Ash may have going on in life. You already know that would never come between the bond you and Jo have," I told her, sitting up so that she could see how serious I was. "Even still, Jo ain't the only person you have. What the hell am I?"

"I don't know what you are, Marcel. I don't—"

"What the hell you mean you don't know what I am?" I asked, feeling offended by that statement.

"You know what I mean, Marcel." She sighed. "I really appreciate you being here for me, and I honestly don't know how I could have gotten through this without you, but it's not the same. Once things get back to being somewhat normal we're going to go back to what we were doing and go our separate ways. Then that still leaves me to figure out what the hell I'm going to do with myself. I've already overstayed my welcome here. It's been over a week, and I haven't done a damn thing but mope around your house crying. I—"

"Shorty, if you were overstaying your welcome, I would have been put your ass out," I told her, trying to lighten the mood.

"Marcel." She sighed again. "You're saying that, but we both know it's about time for me to leave. You have your own life and a whole daughter to be worried about. You don't have time to be trying to baby me too."

"Why can't I baby you both?" I shrugged. "If I'm not complaining, then why are you?"

"Because you don't owe me anything. You're doing this out of pity, and you feel sorry—"

"Girl, gone somewhere with that." I waved her off. "I'm not going to keep telling you the same thing. I'm here because I care, so accept that shit because I'm not going anywhere. You're stuck with me whether you like it or not."

Her stubborn behind was getting ready to continue her argument, but we were interrupted by my ringing phone. Seeing that it was the landlord at Meek's spot, my face frowned in confusion. The landlord rarely ever hit my line if ever. There was no need to. Even with Tameeka being on my shit list, I still paid the rent there every month like clockwork.

"What's up, Mrs. Ross? What's going on?" I answered.

"How are you, Mr. Lane? I know it's kind of early, and I'm sorry to bother you, but I haven't been able to contact Ms. Bryant for a minute now, and I need to know what I should do about the apartment. I know you're still paying the rent, but it's been empty and just sitting here, so—"

"Empty? Hold on," I said, cutting her off. I was confused as hell right now. "What do you mean it's empty?"

"Well, Ms. Lane moved most of her belongings out about two months ago, and I haven't seen her back there since," she cautiously answered. "I'm sorry, Mr. Lane. I thought you were aware of her move."

"Hell no, I wasn't aware," I quipped, trying to reel in my anger. "I'm on my way down there now, Mrs. Ross. Give me a minute."

"What's wrong?" Fatima questioned as she watched me toss the covers from my body and move to my closet.

"I'm about to strangle Meek's ass is what's wrong," I told her, pulling a hoodie over my head. "Aye, throw something on right quick."

"Huh? For what? I can wait here until you get back, Marcel. I'm not trying to be in the middle of y'all's mess again."

"Woman, put some clothes on, and come on," I told her. "We need to finish our little *talk* anyway."

⸙

TAMEEKA THOUGHT SHE WAS SLICK. I HADN'T BOTHERED TO go back by her crib since I went through with Ash and got her to sign the custody papers. I was not sure why I didn't put her behind out in the first place. It was not like she had my seed anymore. I should have let that bird bitch fend for herself.

She had completely wiped out the entire apartment like she actually paid for anything in that bitch. Even the appliances that belonged to the landlord were gone. I didn't know why I didn't expect her to pull some shit like that. It was a whole junky we were talking about.

After settling everything up with Mrs. Ross, I had to get away from there, because the longer I stayed, the more I wanted to go out and find Tameeka. There was no telling what I would do to that damn girl.

"You good?" Fatima asked from the passenger seat as she reached over to rub the back of my hand.

I turned to look at her but didn't speak right away. My head was all over the place right now.

"Marcel?"

"You still fucking with ole' boy?" I bluntly asked.

"Wow." Her eyes bucked as she reared back, shocked by my abruptness. "Where did that come from?"

"It's a simple question, Fatima. Are you, or aren't you?"

"What makes you think that it's even okay for you to ask—"

"Cut the bullshit, man. We're too grown for games, and I'm not about to play them," I told her straight up. "Look, I love yo' ass, Fatima. I've tried to shake that shit, but I can't. I don't even think I want to, but what I'm not about to do is let another

160

bitch play me. That love shit goes out the window then because—"

"Bitch?" She frowned and folded her arms across her chest.

"Is that the only thing you heard me just say?" I asked, getting annoyed. "I'm trying to express my feelings and shit, and you're worried about me calling you a bitch, which by the way, I didn't. I was speaking in general."

Sighing, I ran my hands down my face, contemplating if the conversation was worth continuing. I knew how difficult Fatima could be when she wanted to, but it wasn't the time for that.

"Ma, on some real shit. I want you. No, scratch that. I *need* you," I confessed, turning to look into her eyes so that she could see how serious my words were. "But I can't put myself and my daughter through any more than I already have. I'm a grown ass man, Fatima. I know it took me a minute to grow the hell up, but I know what I want and exactly what I *don't* want. I want to be with you, Fatima. I swear I do, but if you're still on fuck-shit, let me know now so I can treat you accordingly."

I watched her intensely as she soaked in everything I'd just said. Fatima was quiet for so long that I didn't think she was ever going to respond.

"Fatima?"

"Okay, Marcel," she answered simply.

"Okay? What does 'okay' mean? What the hell is *okay*?" I asked, growing frustrated. "Man—"

"Marcel, chill. It means that I hear you, and I understand. We're on the same page, and I swear on my mother that I'm done with Kyle. That's a situation that never should have happened to begin with, and I should have been honest with you from the jump. Again, I'm sorry about that. I know I hurt you, but I want this. I want you and Heaven too. I wouldn't do anything to mess this up if you give us another chance."

"Faye, don't just be saying that shit just to say it. I need you to mean it. You—"

My sentence was cut off by her climbing over the center console and into the driver's seat onto my lap. We were still parked out on the street in front of the apartment building. My windows might have had a dark tint on them, but if someone was being nosy enough, they could simply look straight through the front windshield and see what was going on.

"Girl, what the hell you doing?" I asked but didn't bother stopping her.

"I'm serious, Marcel," she said, staring into my eyes. "I meant every word I said. I want you too, and I want this."

I was not going to lie. I swooned like a little bitch the second she leaned into me and took possession of my lips. It had been so long since I'd tasted her, and I was savoring every second of this moment as I allowed her to have control.

The sound of her growing moans along with the constant grinding she was doing against my manhood, signaled that it was time for me to put a stop to things before things really got out of hand.

"Aight, Faye. Hold on, ma," I said, breaking away from our kiss. "Get back over in your seat. We got time for all that later.

⚜

"MAN, WHAT THE HELL Y'ALL WANT? IS IT 'PULL UP AND GET ON Ash's last nerve' day or something?" Ash grumbled after answering the door with a mug on his face, not bothering to invite us in.

"What the hell wrong with you, fool?" I laughed, closing the door behind Fatima and I and following behind him.

"Yo' mama is what's wrong with me, nigga." He harshly whispered and quickly cast a glance over his shoulder. "I swear,

I love Ma Dukes like she birthed me her damn self, but I'm about two seconds away from spazzing on her ass."

"Nigga, what my mama do to you?" I asked, cracking up laughing.

"She's driving me crazy with this wedding shit. If she shows up at my house one more damn time, waking me up out my good ass sleep, I'm gon'—"

"Do what?"

His eyes squeezed shut at the sound of my mother's voice behind him.

"You gon' do what exactly, Ashley?" she asked with her hands propped on her shapely hips.

"Man, nothing, Ma," he answered, releasing a frustrated breath and rolling his eyes to the ceiling. "I'm going to get back in the damn bed. Y'all can do what y'all want."

"Damn, bruh." I continued laughing after he gave us his ass to kiss and walked away, leaving us all standing there. "It's like that, Ash?"

"He still acting like a big baby?" Jordyn asked, entering into the room.

"What y'all did to my boy, man?" I asked, moving to give Ma Dukes a hug and then Jordyn.

"Nothing. Ashley will be okay," Ma Dukes said, waving him off. "I hope you've come to help us with all this wedding planning, Ms. Fatima."

"Ohhhhh. No wonder he mad," I said, shaking my head. "Y'all in here driving my boy crazy."

"Speaking of craziness," moms started, and I knew some mess was about to follow after she raised her brow in Fatima and my direction. "Have you two cut your bullshit out and worked things out yet?"

"Well, damn. You just gon' come at us like that?"

"You know I don't sugarcoat, Cel. Now, answer my question.

I'm tired of y'all mess," my mama ordered. "Both of you know you're meant to be together, so I don't understand why you keep—"

"Chill, Ma. Dang." I chuckled, pulling Fatima into my side. "You know I'm not about to let her go anywhere. She stuck with me for life."

"Life?" Ma Dukes' eyes lit up, and a cheesy smile spread across her face. "Sounds like we might need to be planning two weddings."

"Hell no," I quickly answered, shutting that idea down. "Slow your roll, woman. We literally just got back together two seconds ago, and you're already trying to send us down the aisle. Marriage ain't nowhere on our radar right now and won't be for awhile."

She shrugged and smirked at us. "You never know, Marcel. Look at Ash and Jordyn."

16

ASH

FOUR MONTHS LATER...

"Aye! Turn the fuck up, man," Marcel yelled out, turning up a bottle of D'usse with one hand and throwing a wad of money at the stripper on stage in front of us. "It's my mother-fuckin' brother's bachelor party!"

That fool was beyond messed up. You would have thought he was the one about to walk down the aisle instead of me. I was letting him have his moment, though. He was convinced that Jordyn was going to have me on straight lockdown, but I kept trying to tell people that Jo's little ass didn't run anything around here.

"Bruh, you better calm yo' ass down. You know Faye don't play that shit," I advised, messing with him.

"Damn. How you gon' try to play me like that? I'm good. Faye already know what's up. Worry about you and yours. My lady's not the one bussing my windows out and setting cars on fire and shit," he replied jokingly, but I didn't find a damn thing funny.

"Nigga, that shit ain't funny," I told him with a straight face. "You know how bad I wanted to drop Jordyn's ass?"

"Hell yeah." He fell over laughing. "I was there. Remember? Good thing you didn't or else you wouldn't be about to walk down the aisle and marry the love of your life tomorrow."

"Love of my life my ass. You just made me mad about that shit all over again." I frowned. "I might just leave her butt standing at the altar tomorrow. Shit, we already married."

"Okay. You go right ahead, and we'll be planning your funeral next. I don't know why you keep playing like you don't know your woman certified crazy. I think she got you beat, bruh. Scratch that. I *know* she do."

I couldn't do anything but shake my head because he was right. My baby wasn't wrapped to tight, but that was probably why we were perfect for each other.

"*Yo! Yo! Yo! Let me cut the beat for a sec,*" I heard the DJ yell over the mic. "We have a very special guest with us tonight! My main man Ash is in the motherfuckin' building!"

As soon as he said my name, the crowd went bananas. You would have thought I was a celebrity up in there. I mean, I kind of was.

"Word around town is that my mans about to tie the knot tomorrow! I need everybody to raise your bottles, your glasses, and whatever the hell else you got in your hands, and salute my nigga!"

I wasn't for having all the attention on me, but I was just going to live in the moment and enjoy myself.

"We have something special planned for the man of the hour," the DJ announced, causing my brow to raise in curiosity. "Yo, Ash, come to the stage for me, bruh."

Glancing over at Marcel, the stupid smirk on his face let me know that he definitely was behind this. Stopping to grab my personal bottle of D'usse from the table, I headed toward the stage to the throne that had been positioned dead in the center and had two strippers flanking both sides. They both took one of my arms and guided me to sit down.

Without warning, the stage lights shut off, and I felt myself being turned around in the chair. My back was facing the crowd, and the curtain was illuminated by a single spotlight.

I wasn't too sure about what was about to go down, but I didn't do well with surprises. Discreetly easing my hand under my shirt, I let it rest on my piece as I waited for the curtain to open.

"Private Show" by T.I. began to blast through the speakers, causing me to smile inwardly. It was one of Jordyn's favorite songs. It was funny how she was constantly on my mind, and the smallest things had me missing her like crazy.

I was so caught up with my thought of Jordyn that I hadn't even realized that the curtain had opened, revealing a single pole in the middle of the stage. A figure appeared, but I couldn't see anything but their silhouette until they came to stand directly in front of me. The large mask the woman wore disguised her features, hiding her face from the crowd. She had my undivided attention. My eyes zeroed in on her thick chocolate thighs as she sauntered over to me and stopped between my open legs.

Her tiny hands gripped onto my thighs as she leaned into me and pressed her chest into mine. Her lips came to my ear, and I thought she was about to speak. Instead, she quickly dipped the tip of her tongue inside my ear and stepped away. She sent some kind of signal to the two chicks still standing beside me, and they nodded and pushed my seat closer to the pole on the stage.

I had seen my fair share of strippers perform in my life, but none held my attention like that one did. I was not sure if it was the alcohol or just the excitement of the night, but I was all into it. My eyes followed her up the pole until she made it to the very top and widened at the sight of her dropping all the way down until she landed into a full split.

Baby had some skills on her. The way she worked her hips to the beat had a nigga mesmerized. I could hear the rest of the crowd going crazy behind me and dollars were flying everywhere as they watched her work her ass all over me. She was putting in some major work. I wasn't ready for it to be over, but the song had come to an end, and she was already rushing back behind the curtain before I had time to react.

Hopping up from my seat, I hurried behind her so that I could catch her before she managed to get away.

"Damn, ma. What's the rush?" I asked after catching up to her and approaching her from behind.

"Because the show's over, playboy," she answered with her back still to me.

"It doesn't have to be," I said, moving into her personal space and bringing my lips to her ear. "That lil' show you put on out there was nice, but I'm more interested in a *private* party."

"I don't do private parties, sweetheart," she said, trying to maneuver around me, but I stopped her by sliding my arm around her waist and leading us toward one of the doors in the back.

"Aren't you about to get married?" she asked, stumbling over her words.

"And?" I returned, kissing down her neck. "What's your point?"

"My point is you got me fucked up," she barked, ripping the mask from her face and whipping around with her hand ready to strike me.

I caught it mid-air and snatched her to me. "What type of gullible nigga do you take me for, Jo?" I smirked down at her.

"How'd you know it was me?"

"I know that body from anywhere, ma. Besides, *he* spotted you first," I told her, pressing my hard erection into her midsection. "Told you my dick only gets hard for you, shorty."

"Yeah, whatever," she said, trying to push me away from her. "Did you at least enjoy it?"

"Hell yeah. Why you think I'm back here trying to get an encore?"

"Because you thought you were about to come back here and slide up in some nasty stripper bitch," she said, pretending to be mad.

"Girl, don't play with me," I told her, smacking her hard on her plump ass. "Oh, and don't think your ass ain't in trouble either."

"What I do?" she asked innocently.

"You out here half-naked, shaking yo' ass in front of that packed ass club for the whole world to see."

"I wasn't paying any of those people any attention," she said, sliding her arms around my neck. "I was dancing for my husband and my husband only."

"Well, your husband's trying to slide up in those guts, so what's up lil' mama? What you trying to do?"

"Whatever you trying to do, daddy," she answered, easing down to the floor until she was in a crouching position.

Her eyes lit up with mischief as she eyed my erection. One of her hands came up, and she began to caress me through my jeans. She had my pants undone and down around my ankles before I could blink. Jordyn wasted no time taking me into her mouth and swallowing my dick whole.

"Gah damn, girl! Shit, Jo!" I hissed, grabbing a fistful of her hair that she'd straightened. It was flowing down her back. "We doing it like that, shorty?"

The way she was sliding my dick in and out of her mouth was driving me insane. Her lips clamped down, and she suctioned hard every time she got to the head before she popped it from her mouth and put it right back in, swallowing me again.

I glanced down and almost nutted instantly at the sight of her playing in her pussy as she pleasured me. She was soaking her fingers up something serious, and my mouth watered at the thought of tasting her juices.

Stepping out of her grasp, I smirked at the slight whimper that come from her lips when I pulled her up from the floor. Taking the hand that was inside of her, I brought her finger up to my nose and took a long whiff of her scent before taking them into my mouth and sucking them clean.

"Bend over," I ordered in a husky voice.

"But I wasn't done—"

Spinning her around and pushing her torso forward, I pushed her down until her hands were touching the floor. "What did I say?" I asked, smacking her ass and watching it ripple. "Grab hold to your ankles, ma."

Ripping off the thin material that she was wearing, my eyes traveled over her entire body, causing me to lick my lips. The high stilettos that she wore had her ass sitting up just right, and I had the perfect view of her glistening entrance. Running the head of my dick over her clit, I moved it back and forth until her juices coated me.

"Baby," Jordyn called, breathing hard.

I knew that she was growing impatient and was ready for me to put us both out of our misery. Positioning myself at her opening, I slowly entered her sanctuary and didn't stop until I hit rock bottom.

"Oh God," she moaned out. Her hand shot back to grab my wrist.

Pulling her up until her back was pressed into my chest, I dug deeper until she screamed out.

"You know I love you?"

"Fuck me, Ashley. Please, fuck me, baby," she begged.

"Answer my question, Jordyn," I growled, slamming hard into her once. "Do you know I love you?"

"Yes! Yes, baby! I know! I love you too!" she cried out.

"Good," I said, pushing her back down to the floor. "*Now,* I'll fuck you."

✥✥✥

A HAND LANDED ON MY SHOULDER AND EYES TRAVELED UP the length of the arm, landing on a face that I wasn't expecting to see.

"You ready, big bro?" Dylan asked, smiling hard at me. "Today's the big day."

"I was born ready, lil' nigga," I answered and turned to pull him into a tight embrace. "What you doing here, man?"

"What you mean? Did you honestly think we would miss your wedding, man? Hell, I never thought this day would ever happen." Dylan laughed.

"You and me both, D," a voice called out from behind us.

I turned to face Morgan, and we both stood staring at each other without uttering a word. It was he who broke our staring match first and moved to pull me into his arms. I don't care how hard I was. I missed my damn brothers, and it fucked with me every day that we weren't on speaking terms.

"I wasn't expecting y'all to be here, man," I said after we finally pulled away.

"You know your lady wasn't having that shit," Morgan said. "Aye, Ash, you know I ain't no punk or no shit like that, but Jordyn's ass spooks me. She threatened a nigga and everything. There was no way we could *not* be here."

We all laughed at that, and I could just imagine Jordyn

trying to boss up on Morgan's big behind. My baby was fearless and didn't take shit from anybody.

"So you only came because my lady threatened you?" I laughed.

"That, and there was no way in hell I was about to miss my brother and best friend in the entire world's wedding," he said, looking into my eyes. "I love you, man, and I'm proud of you, Ashley. I mean that."

"I love you, too, bro." I nodded, trying to keep my emotions at bay. "Okay. That's enough of all this sentimental shit. Let's go before Cello's moms start yelling about me not being in place."

"Let's get this show on the road then," Morgan said, slapping a hand onto my shoulder. "My nigga's getting married!"

❦

"How you feeling, Mrs. Thomas?" I asked Jordyn after she plopped down next to me.

Pulling her feet onto my lap, I removed her shoes and began to massage her feet. I knew they had to be killing her. She and Fatima had been up dancing nonstop since the reception started. I was surprised she was taking a break now.

"Amazing," she answered, leaning in to place a kiss on my lips. "Everything turned out so perfect."

"Yeah, it did. You and Ma Dukes did the damn thing," I told her, looking around the venue again.

If Ma ever wanted to pick up a hobby, a wedding planning business was definitely for her. She worked my last nerves over the last few months, but it was worth it. She'd managed to plan Jordyn's dream wedding and brought all of her visions to life in barely no time.

"You about danced out yet?" I jokingly asked.

"Nope." She giggled. "Just thought I'd come over here to see how my husband was doing."

"I'm Gucci, baby girl. Just been enjoying the view." I smirked, winking at her. "You looking a lil' thick in that dress."

She removed her feet from my lap and stood, glancing behind her at her backside. "I think you're right, babe. I might have you to blame for that," she said, pulling a small box out of nowhere and tossing it at me.

"Oh, so you got me a gift?"

"Yep," she answered and walked away without waiting for me to open it.

The sneaky look Jordyn cast my way over her shoulder sparked my curiosity and had me anxious to find out what was in the box. The second my eyes landed on the contents, my eyes bucked, and I shot to my feet.

"Don't fucking play with me, Jordyn!" My deep voice boomed, startling our guests and causing them to look my way in horror. "Is this for real?"

She nodded, biting her lip to hide her smile as she stood in the center of the dance floor. I rushed to her and swooped her up the air, squeezing her to my body.

"Ow, Ashley! Put me down! You're squishing me." She giggled, trying to free herself from my hold.

"Man, I don't care about all that. Ma, you're really carrying my seed?" I asked again, still unsure if the news was real. "Like for real, for real?"

"Yes, Ashley. For real, for real." She nodded, laughing at me. "We're having a baby."

"That's what I'm talking about!" I yelled, pumping my fist into the air. "Y'all this woman is about to have my baby!"

"Oh my God!" Fatima yelled from nearby and rushed to us. "You're pregnant, Jo? My baby's about to have a baby, y'all!"

The entire place had erupted in cheers as everyone took

turns congratulating us. My only focus was on my beautiful wife, who was about to be the mother of my child. I never would have thought that I would experience the type of joy that I was feeling at that very moment.

After all the bullshit that I had been through and all the dirt I'd done in my past, I didn't think that a happy life was possible for a nigga like me. Jordyn proved me wrong, though. She had bullied her way into my life and heart. She made me the happiest man on earth, and I didn't think she even realized it. It was a good thing I decided to spare her life that first night we crossed paths. Jordyn had managed to do the impossible and tamed the savage.

Join our mailing list to get a notification when Leo Sullivan Presents has another release!

Text LEOSULLIVAN to 22828 to join!
To submit a manuscript for our review, email us at submissions@leolsullivan.com

CPSIA information can be obtained
at www.ICGtesting.com
Printed in the USA
LVHW082208221118
597793LV00037B/401/P

9 781730 947070